OUR
MACHINERY

a novel by

Thaïs Miller

(BrownpaperpublishinG)

First Printing

ISBN: 978-1-43821-126-8

Published By Brown Paper Publishing

www.brownpaperpublishing.net
www.predicatemag.com

Printed in the United States of America

Acknowledgements

My thanks are due first and foremost to my parents for their love, encouragement, patience, and advice. Thanks are also due to the faculty of the American University Literature Department (including Kermit Moyer, Matt Getty, and Randon Noble) for their encouragement during the writing process. I would also like to thank Dr. Robert Johnson for his generosity. "May the words of my mouth and the prayer of my heart be acceptable to you, O Lord" (Psalm 19:15).

To 'You'

OUR
MACHINERY

...Machine...

A Machine was invented that sucked human bodies up like slugs and converted their bodies (and their subsequent deaths) into energy.

It was invented by a man named Albert DiGennero, who went to one of the three top Ivies (Princeton, Yale, or Harvard). He went to whichever one was the top Ivy League school at the time (those three always argued, rotated, and competed for the top spot). He was already white-haired and balding with a greasy comb-over (with a life of its own) when, sitting in his lab one day, he decided to get back at humanity for all the terrible things people had done to him (called him names in Grammar School, teased him for his brilliance). He didn't have a lot of time left, so what did he care about how he spent the rest of it? Childless and alone, he didn't care much about leaving a legacy or some sort of improvement in the world. All he wanted was his name and a diagram in a mainstream Biology Textbook, outlining *How the great Dr. DiGennero converted Dead Human Flesh into Energy.* That's how he'd make his mark and seek revenge on all those scientists mocking his earlier work (not to mention those evil playground kids who never picked him for kickball). No, the world would never be the same after his great invention. *So let them eat themselves*, he figured. He wanted people to die in their own stupidity,

9

drown in their own feces. It took years for Dr. DiGennero to reconfigure and modify the old Slug Model into a Human Consumption Machine; each new part and lever making death even more painful and the electrical energy drawn out of it even stronger.

Dr. DiGennero decided to administer the first test (on a small scale of course) on his foot. He wrote his observations in his scientific notebook:

The fat knuckle of the big toe bends under the front of the toe, as though a marble was caught under its nail and settled, lodged there unmoving. The toe looks more like a thumb, separated and larger from the rest of the piggies. The smallest toe has literally folded into itself as the other, longer toes dangle in mid-air, twitching, trying to break free from the mass of skin sticking them together, trapping them like amber. The toes smell like cedar tree-sap, convulsing against the body of the foot. Look at these toes. They are imprisoned by skin, an ugly, malicious, prison master, a sadistic toe with a hunch over its arches. It is a hunchback prison guard, the smaller toes his inmates. The toes try to scream for help, but they have no mouths to scream with. But who would listen to toe screams anyway? Perhaps the toes were mad even before they were put under the treatment of the first model. Why is that ugly foot shooting out so awkwardly from my ankle? It is as if it wants to show off the hidden deformity under the halo of genius, the abnormality under the skin, now on top. Was it ever truly hidden under the surface?

Those piggies, those fat, yellow lumps of skin: hoofs. I will trudge along on them. If I walk barefoot all day, the large calluses under my foot will start bleeding and smell like salty, stale, burnt leaves. Drip. Oil from my skin is dripping, burning, and scalding the panel I placed it on. The oil boils, glistens, corrodes, and churns, coils, slides, slithers. The droplets squirm like amoebas.

If those toes could speak, they would yell out in scattered, delusional tongues. The big toe would yell back words of depravity to get them to shut up, beating them down with his words, like a night stick. The little toes loathe that prison guard toe. The big toe fears the marble stuck in its hull. All sadists are insecure. The little toes want freedom, the big toe wants to enjoy their pain, it wants to torture and harass the little toes, especially the baby stub. It wants them to suffer until they all decay and fall off, black and purple with boils, until they are dead.

Now, the foot itself has lost all its natural beauty, that holy icon of life. It doesn't twinkle as it sashays across the floor. The experiment is a success. It is dead.

But that was just the beginning. Dr. DiGennero created a large scale Machine, one that could convert a full body, then two, then five, then fifteen. This Machine would solve all energy problems. That was it; that was the only excuse the Machine needed to gain wide acceptance and acclaim from the community. Ethics were no question, who cared if a few died while the rest of the world lived comfortably? Sure, there would be Machiavellian sacrifices, but for the greater good. With more energy, from a bottomless source, the problems of the world could be solved. No more energy crisis, no more blackouts (the environment would be kept intact, while solving issues of over-population). Dr. DiGennero presented his work at conferences around the country. Slowly but surely, the word spread and the little known scientist won the Nobel Prize for his research. The international scientific community applauded his work.

Dr. DiGennero's foot was amputated and his doctors found that a cancer from the foot spread to his ankle. The cancer, slowly creeping up his leg, would surely kill him. It was time for him to sell his idea, leave something to this world in physicality, not just an idea in text books. He got some big-name buyers next to his hospital bed, first the major computer and software companies then some lower-level insurance corporations. The multinational corporations were all over him. They wanted to keep their businesses alive; everyone needed energy to continue to be a fast-paced commodity (Heaven knows that oil and gasoline were down the drain). Electricity was on big companies' brains. They craved it for their investors, for their consumers. Money, money; had to get some. By the time DiGennero died, several companies were fighting over the rights; and then the government got a sniff of the stuff and wanted in.

The government wouldn't leave this technology (non-pollutant, cost-effective energy) to private corporations. Imagine the consequences of having a completely free market. No, no, instead of having to make a million laws preventing individual profit gain, why not just get in on the earnings and make money for the government itself? So, the government monopolized the industry and hired private businesses to manufacture and run the machines. Large plants were built throughout most states in the country, within a two-mile radius of most federal buildings. The businesses hired the same blue-collar workers attending to steel and coal mines to build these People Eating Machines.

Although originally nameless, two fat male engineers, while mass manufacturing the product, nicknamed the Machine *Big Sexy*. It's a funny story: The two brothers, Rufus and Julius Ignora, were standing next to a large, hatch door examining the many long, oval blades as they tore into a mechanical conveyer belt. As the blades ripped over the belt (a flaw of their particular model) chemical residue spurted out and caught on Julius's rubber pant-leg. The toxic, acidic chemicals started to chew through the rubber material, forcing Julius to strip his clothing and Rufus started to laugh.

Ha! Oh man! You got a hard on!

Looking down, Julius realized that he became enthralled in the excitement of the moment; the ripping of the belt, like some ancient rape scene converted into a modern, perverse, mechanical disaster. He imagined the night Rufus took him out to have a picnic with the town slut-turned-prostitute. How no one entered that park because of all the homelessness and debauchery there. Both fully-clothed men ripped open the girl's flimsy white blouse; he remembered how their bodies, like the food in the picnic basket, unraveled, unwrapped, fell onto the ground (breaking open, smashing together, juices spreading in a myriad of directions). Rufus and Julius joked about how this was so much better than reading the soft porn they had become accustomed to. While usually deprived of their greater, carnal desires, they were finally able to Get It Up at this type of employment.

They looked at each other only to reflect that what they truly wanted (rape, homoerotic incest) was not allowed. How something about the screeching noises, flashes of hot light, and smell of burnt rubber made them horny. Rufus thought of the freedom (not like you or I think of freedom, of men without machines telling them what to do, but the freedom to destroy things). They wanted the freedom to live without morals or principles in a world where modernity allows anything to happen. They envisioned the type of freedom that's served on a silver platter to a fat man in a lazy-boy chair. Rufus thought of creating a deadly computer virus that festered into unsuspecting computers, killing not only the machines, but the people using them. No, no, he thought more directly of throwing a brand-new, flat screen TV out of a tenth story window, hitting a business man on the way down, the silver, shattered pieces complementing the shimmering red on the side walk. Oh the carnage. Julius thought of a high speed car chase in a brand new Cadillac on a multi-lane highway; the gears shifting, the power exerted over speed and place. Then a giant truck smashes into it (glittering pieces of plastic and metal contort the moist bodies inside). Rufus brought up video games, blood splattering the screen (how he wished it was real blood). He imagined an anarchical world, in which he could run around lawless without morals or rules. (And people say that video games have no effects on real life?) Julius thought of roller coasters, then of a hang-gliding ride at an amusement park near their home. The ride's intent was to make the boys experience each aspect of hang-gliding, using every sense (even the smell of evergreen below). Julius imagined the ride breaking, his body hurtling towards the chaos below (his body submerged) his sweat, his heartbeat, all senses artificially tenderized. Finally, they were creating a Machine for that. Yes. Big Sexy was what they would call it, the climactic high and the ultimate orgasm. The name spread. And often, employers would find their workers masturbating to the Machines. If only they knew that the engineers in their white collars were doing the same. Gingerly stroking their laptops and car dashboards, watching animated porn on a flat, widescreen TV; the same perverted undertones the blue-collar workers were experiencing was happening in the same way, on a different level.

Since then, the Machine had an odd reputation. If just looking at the carnage of the machine made someone horny, the actual experience of it killing someone must have had the effect, ten fold. Rumor had it that the painful sensation inflicted by the Machine as it killed and absorbed energy (converting it to its own electricity) was erotic. That somehow, as the Machine sucked the life out of a man's juicy organs, he would feel the greatest pain and pleasure possible in a lifetime. Little scientific fact substantiated this claim (but many were curious to test it).

First and foremost, the machines craved human flesh, so businesses realized that they needed volunteers. Businesses just needed a label, some pretty, pink wrapping to cover up the debris inside, something that would sell; something that would inspire people to sacrifice their bodies. The businesses ran telethons, inspiring consumers with the advertisement that this Machine would *Reverse Global Warming And Solve Problems With Population Control* and that Citizens *Can Work Hands-On To Directly Affect Change* and most of all, this will *Provide Energy* so that *Anyone Who Volunteers Will Be A Productive Member Of Society, Contributing To The Greater Good*. Little did consumers know that *they* would be consumed.

The first to go were the old widows (the primary victims of telethons) who longed to get out of the house for a new form of productive philanthropy. Overnight, wrinkled hands, sweet smiles, and over-active libidos clutched their enlarged archaic phones, taking their sweet time dialing, feeling each key, because their blind eyes could no longer distinguish their finger tips from the numbers. These widows would clamor for their chance to give back to humanity, and get an extra kick on the side. What a way to go, kill two birds with one stone (give back to humanity and get that last, glistening fuck, the most wonderful, to make their passing just a bit better, to feel fulfilled at last). Their trembling voices muted by the pricking teeth grinning on the other end. They had nothing else to lose, argued the government representatives, who cheered at reduced Social Security spending. Businesses even offered their employees increased benefits if they signed waivers committing to Retirement By Machine (ending their lives through Big Sexy instead of by retiring, and, notably, in place of receiving a pension).

After more enhanced, descriptive rumors of the machine's nickname spread, next to go were the sadists and masochists (dying for the ultimate, sensually-painful experience, literally). Around the corners of the cinder-block factories, dominatrix play-things could be seen, whip in hand, waiting to end it all. A thin, coal-haired woman wearing all leather with a leash attached to a fat man in a dog collar smiled resiliently against the sky, defying the system she deviated from, fitting into their color scheme at last. But still, there had been no survivors and therefore no first-hand reports of the Machine actually inducing an orgasmic sensation. The Machine's factual feeding process seemed quite the opposite. The process was, in fact quite tediously wrenching and long, consisting of a loud, humming drone throughout and terrible smells of battery acid. Slowly grinding and mashing up the bodies (feet first), disintegrating any useless parts with a special acid, etc. took up to forty-eight hours. There was no anesthesia; why give it to someone who was bound to die anyway?

After this news came out, the next to volunteers were

suicidal maniacs, people desperate for *any* feeling (because they felt empty most of their lives), longing for death and pain on the way. I'm sure the boiling chemicals pumped into their organs filled them with something. The government therefore installed a Euthanasia Program, liberally allowing what people had been bellowing for, years prior. In response, those dying of terminal illnesses jumped on the bandwagon.

The government got rid of welfare (those who were impoverished and in massive debt were arrested like never before). The justice system incorporated the Machine into rudimentary punishments. Soon, small-time drug offenders were on a new type of death row. And people convicted of just being poor without a government to care for their needs joined them.

Could you believe it? I couldn't. Reality and Truth spread like wild-fire, exposed to a dry breeze. Nothing these people heard deterred them from allowing the Machine to become ingrained into our society. Humans needed Machines, not other humans. Politicians serve man, don't they? They give people want they want. If the democratic majority of people were dumb enough to support this Machine, did that mean that it was all for the greater good? All the while, it left me to wonder, was it more victorious to fight or just give in?

I just couldn't accept that man was so malicious in nature.

Seeing how I was already a dissident from proper society (a penniless artist, in no way Being Productive or Advancing Society, according to the government) I decided that I would fight the mass slaughter and save humanity from itself.

The first thing I did was try to deplete the Machine's source of energy. I widely distributed birth control (condoms, diaphragms, and the infamously prescribed Pill) for six months. I found that not only were people still producing babies (the wheat of the flour) but in even greater numbers, now that they knew if they couldn't keep the baby, they could always donate or contribute their baby to the Machine. When government caught on to the Murder Label the Machine was receiving, the government exploited the Machine's deadly nature and sold it as the new birth control. This would be *Less Costly And Less Emotionally Damaging* (not to mention more productive) *Than Abortion Or Adoption.* One couple was quoted as saying, Hey, as long as our TV and microwave keep running, who needs protection? The government advertised the cost-effectiveness of this procedure of slaughtering newborn babies in their famous advertisement *A New Wing To The House Or An Active Way Of Conserving Energy... Give Back To The Community*. The government made Murder the new Recycle. Why have people, when we have a regime? If the average Joe was ignorant and going to die anyway, why not use him in a productive way to solve all the government's Intellectual energy problems? The government couldn't run on empty, it needed some type of fuel.

In reaction, I saw only one thing that I could do: kidnap newborn babies and raise them on my own, for fear their parents would redistribute energy through them. As long as I protected innocence, I could raise these babies into a pacifistic army to one day revolt against the heinous crimes of the government. I would teach these babies love and peace, telling them that their mission in life was Not To Be Productive. These babies were not Machines; they did not have to fulfill a purpose that would serve the rather misguided desires of humanity. Ads in magazines said *Reproduce The New Way* a way feeding directly into our electrical outlets and computer screens. See how definitions can be contorted full circle in this world (as long as words are used to a regime's advantage).

So I tried to steal one baby. I dressed like a nurse with the nametag *Rumpelstiltskin*. While holding one small baby, I came within five feet of the hospital exit before I was almost arrested. *Almost*. I escaped by putting the baby on the counter and claiming that I was a covert government inspection officer Just Peeking At The New Crop—the latest nutrients to be harvested by the Machine downtown. Can you believe that they bought that? They didn't even bat an eye. They even let me touch the baby more to determine how much energy could be made out of it. City people, how they love their Machines; those sexy industrialized wastelands. Watch any car commercial and what do you see? Big city, sexy driver, shiny leather interior—another Machine attracting the human libido.

I needed to escape, to survive, to rescue those idiots drooling over interior design magazines, home-shopping networks, and titillated by the latest online coupon. I had to save the consumers from consuming themselves.

The leaves were quickly falling from the trees, like tourists rushing onto subway trains, their distinct colors lost in a rushing haze of yellow, red, brown. They all mixed together, dying together, falling together. I looked on the ground and a beetle crawled out from a crackling brown leaf. The leaf made a print, like an ink stamp on the pavement. The bug hustled its shiny body past the underbelly of the leaf, into the afternoon sunlight, creeping its way past the cinnamon imprint, escaping from the trap of the moment. The sun blurred into the skyline, creating that beautiful pink time of day (the most surreal part of every day). I heard a mockingbird. I dread mockingbirds. Their noise always reminds me that it's the end of the day. They always make me aware that something is dying, that time is fleeting, that my time is slowly fading away. Those mockingbirds tell me that the paranoia of the night is going to commence soon. Run; I had to run back to my home, before the night enclosed me, before I was lost in its bleak shadows.

My home was a small apartment located near a bakery. Well, it was a bakery until it was torn down in place of a two-in-one combo: a Machine and a Machine factory. Machine Factory. Machines producing other Machines. This was progress? This was supposed to be the modern advancement of man? But man wasn't doing anything. I used to buy food from the bakery. It was yummy. After the Machine was built, I would watch people line up along the sidewalk waiting to die. They were distracting and not producing lovely smells. Most of them smelled like they had wet themselves in line. Their faces were pale in the moonlight, and even paler in the rush of morning. I loved mornings until the Machine was built near my home. Then, I would dread them. Because every morning I would wake up, feel calm and collected, just happy to be alive, smiling, and then I would look out my window: the business man, coffee still in hand, wearing the latest executive-member tie given out by the club, stands in line, like the others, still clutching his briefcase (it is not filled with office papers, but sweet remembrances and bank statements he wants to take with him to the afterlife, a note from his girlfriend in college, the one that committed suicide, a picture of his dog that died when he was nine, a video of his diseased mother singing to him in his crib). These remembrances would be stashed, with the others, in a side room to the main Machine chamber. Stories of the inner workings of the Machine spread not through the mouths of those who committed themselves, but from the workers, who boasted about the latest finds in some of these rooms. One found a book of psalms, another a golden watch (and the craziest find, an embalmed poodle). And as these remembrances of love and humanity were discarded like loose bills in a pocket book of a millionaire, so would this man's body be boiled, burned, and grated (creating the worst smell in the world, the smell of burnt pubic hairs, flesh, fat and oil). Like the rest of the people in line, he would be considered contributing to the greater good, and my skin would crawl as I looked at him. I would not drink coffee that morning; I would stare blankly out my window, unable to ignore the dozens of people lined up, unable to ponder, to wonder What's going through their heads? How can they think it is justified to do this? What are they thinking as they wait (as they fill out bureaucratic papers releasing their lives to a corporate-government complex, to the Machine behind the Machine)? No, all thoughts would ooze from the pores of my skull, leaving me brain dead as I focused on their lifeless faces. My coffee cup would smash against my wooden floor like the leaves against the pavement, desperately trying to make a lasting imprint, only to be removed by the dust and the wind.

Ring.

John the painter called. You never met John, so I'll try to recreate him best I can, so you can get a better impression.

Are you alright? His voice was raspy in the mornings, as if he had a voice box implanted in his throat.

No, I answered.

You can't let this kill you; it's already killing so many others. You have to live, despite the deaths. Just to prove the Machine wrong. Just to exist in spite of the carnage.

You live. What do you do? You don't have a Machine next to your house; you don't see the lines outside all through the mornings, all through the evenings. People lining up because of its popularity. What can I do to live if they die? I die with them.

No, John said. You are smarter than them. You will live despite them.

I will be like the old woman on Masada, who must live as the sole-survivor, to tell the tale of the suicides because it will be so late in my life that I will die soon anyway. Except, there are no Romans. Or are the Romans the energy? Are the Romans the energy as western society?

Stop! Just stop. I'm coming over.

John was quiet. He entered the room wearing a sweater, a scarf, and a knit hat I made for him one year with some gray and brown string. He loved that hat. He slowly unraveled the red scarf and placed it upon the wooden coat-rack at the entry way. It was as if with each article of clothing he stripped, he tried to reveal himself to me (as if he would make this place holy, he would make this a sanctuary, a place of truth). I could recognize him now. The grooves in his face were familiar, abandoned by the earthly covers of modernity. He took off the hat, revealing his messed black hair (he had been scratching at his head at night, violently probing his brain for an answer to the pain and empathy he felt). He hadn't slept well. Finally, he stripped the warm sweater and looked at me sadly. I stood by the window in panties with a glass of water. You will ask Half Full or Half Empty? You will see.

Don't just stand like that, John said. Watching *them*. He walked closer toward me, staring at my chilled breasts and messed hair, red eyes.

The widow's open, you must be freezing, he said. And he shut them. He put his arms around my cold body (a hand on my left breast and another on my right hip).

I am a sculpture, Pygmalion. Won't you carve some warmth in me? I imagined him painting purple circles around my nipples, drawing on each ligament, brushing his paints against my skin (some feeling, the tickle of the brush against the freckles on my arms, something).

You're going crazy in here.

And you're not? I snapped back, looking directly at his cheek next to my face.

I can't watch you standing here.

Then let's go out and do something about this. I can't stand idly by.

John walked behind me; he placed his mouth on my shoulder, gently soothing his chapped lips on my skin. I stood still, watching John (the artist at work).

We have friends, he told me. We have resources. We'll go out into the community and be the first ones to fight this thing.

I turned my head and he licked my neck.

You're smart, he told me. You tell me who to get together and what we'll do. We'll have a convention.

What should we call it?

Not all movements need names.

His hand relaxed down, removing the last thing covering me.

We got together other artists. Megda (the freckled, red-haired Midwestern poet) Evan (the blonde with brown eyes) Fredrick (the graphic artist) Gregor and Shina (the performing artists) Shawn (the abstract artist, painter-sculptor extraordinaire) Emily and Kyle (the short musicians who refused to wear socks) Henry (the painter who refused to wear sandals or shoes at all for that matter. And together, our liberal, intelligent, creative minds created a convention to start fighting the Machine. And people say that Art doesn't affect Society.

So, I got together other artists to draw huge Apocalyptic Disaster Pieces comparing the Machine to a non-discriminatory Genocide (then just any Cide, Suicide, Infanticide, etc). Until finally we coined the term *Machineocide* (Death By Machine). This time, however, Death By Machine wasn't referred to as a penalty (although the government instituted Machineocide for convicts on death row and imprisoned enemy combatants to light up computer screens last spring, without informing the public).

Why wasn't anyone else doing something to stop the madness?

Then, we decided to transfer our focus onto television sitcoms, because TV was such a hot commodity. Our show's premise was that a family living in the future had to deal with the perils of what seemed to be an At-Home, Make-Your-Own Machineocide. There were moments such as when Kevin was restrained from converting his sister Suzy into battery fluid.

Mommy? What's homicide?

That's when you put someone in the Machine that you like.

But I don't like Suzy at all!

It was complicated, at first, intricately weaving some realistic stories into a fictitious world. Whoever thought social commentary could be so artistic? The surreal became realistic and the realistic became surreal. We posted these episodes as video clips online, until we got major TV networks to sign on to the project (giving us a one-season contract). Nobody minded how radical our ideas were; they just thought that it was Science Fiction (and Science Fiction can't change people's minds or provoke social change, right? It's merely entertainment). There wasn't supposed to be any greater meaning behind anything.

Our second major network show was about a group of intelligent people who volunteered to live inside a hygienic bubble, to be studied by scientists in the outside world. The people inside of the bubble were conscious of life only within the bubble and remained oblivious to outer-world conditions. One day, the researchers on the outside all died of an infectious disease that was slowly but surely eating away at the greater population. A scientist from the outside manages to tell the people inside the bubble. Our questions were these: How would they deal with it? Would they believe the news? Would they be indifferent to the deaths of the people outside their comfortable ecosystem? Or would they actually miss them? Would they stay in the bubble forever? Or go outside and fight the disease to save humanity?

We created spin-offs to our shows (one in which everyone in society got plastic surgery, took psychotropic drugs, and of course, ate and bought the same clothes made by starving, over-worked children, so they could all look alike and subsequently think identical thoughts). It was hilarious. And the viewers loved it. Our show received some of the network's highest ratings. Another spin-off was about really fat people who ate all of the world's food, until there was nothing left for anyone else. It hit Number One in Prime Time. Our infamous group of writers, story designers, and collaborating artists got first pick of the best time slots. The last show we made was about how everyone played a certain videogame to escape real life. However, the videogame had factual consequences in reality. For example, if two players had sex in the game, they had sex in real life and had to deal with a subsequent pregnancy. If someone killed someone else in the game, the victim was killed in reality. The players soon had to make life inside the game-world as structured as in actuality in order to survive the chaos and destructive nature of humanity. We won an Emmy.

After television, we decided to move into film. We made artsy underground cult films. Our films were mostly documentaries, recording the destruction of the Machine. We interviewed family members of some of the original volunteers. People left our movies with chills, but then resumed their normal routines the next day (just feeling a little bit queasy). I wonder what would have happened if we exposed workers of the Machines to these tapes. But they were probably immune to the grotesque reality of their work already. It wasn't like *A Clockwork Orange*, where we could strap them down, hold open their eyelids, and administer a serum telling them what pain to empathize with (telling them what was Bad and Good in this world). Government advertising was already doing that for us. No. People still had the free choice to hate one another and to kill each other; apparently, because it was so propelled, endorsed, and motivated by the government.

We made posters and put them up around major cities and some smaller suburbs; we produced Top Ten sitcoms on TV, only to find that our First Amendment ad-campaign (and especially our pride in signing our outspoken artwork) labeled us Enemies Of The State and made it easier for the government to catch Shawn and John (the

Jackson Pollacks of our time) and convict them (sentencing their free words to the Machine murder they fought so hard against, the death prescribed for so many other patriots). Well, maybe not Patriots, anymore. Is a Patriot someone who loves the foundational beliefs of a county? (i.e. the Bill Of Rights and the Constitution) or someone who changes and molds to conform to current government beliefs? If not a Patriot, he was at least a Savior Of Humanity (my Savior; he never told the government about my or any of our coworkers' involvement) seeing as how the government was against, not for, us in the end.

  I watched John line up outside the Machine from my apartment window. He looked up to find me. Emily had already given him enough narcotics so that he wouldn't feel a thing going into it. She snuck it through a courtesy package during the trial, just in case anything ever happened. I watched him lined up with Shawn. I watched John's black eyes stare down the sunrise as his feet crackled against the leaves on the sidewalk (he was only nine steps away from the entrance). I opened my window and I dropped a glass of water. It crashed on the ground below. And the line of Machine Volunteers moved away from the side of my apartment building. They weren't afraid to die, but they were afraid of a little water? Never mind the shards of glass. I stuck my head out the window and John looked up toward me. I wanted him to see me, not what society had trapped me in, not the box around me. I wanted him to see what he had always seen inside, beyond all that. I stuck my head out that window and he looked at me, his eyes tearing. I imagined the very cells of clarity in his brain, seeping through the membrane of his skull, of the skin, dripping beads of their essence onto the surface of his forehead, like a glistening crown. I stepped out onto the ledge, my body not supported by anything on the inside. I didn't care that I could fall. I didn't care, because I knew John had already fallen. I took off my clothes, piece by piece (first the shoes, then the socks, the sweater, unzipped the pants). I took off everything, until I was nude and cold, standing on the ledge outside my window. The people gawked at the nude girl parading from the side of the apartment building.

  Get off of there! an old man from the line yelled. You'll kill yourself.

  Would you rather I was nude in there? I motioned toward the building. And John stared at me as I stared into his eyes. Droplets of his soul oozed out of him as I imagined the visions in front of him that would pierce his head. I wanted him to paint me with his eyes as the globs of tears stained his own canvas.

Paint me!

But I've already painted you! he cried out. My mind has painted you.

I envisioned his brushes caressing my skin. People shook their heads and thought that we were nuts. We received evil glances from people who had decided to commit suicide for their own selfish purposes. Converting your body into energy is not a form of self-sacrifice; it is a form of self-mutilation for respect in our society and loathsome prestige from the government. These people were not part of some greater cause. They wanted the fame and glory, like any of the rest of us. I didn't watch them after a while, my mind so fixed, so concentrated on my last moments with John. I imagined his hands holding me still, supporting me on the ledge so that I would not fall (so that I would not descend like the rest of them). The smell of dogwood filled the air.

Most people didn't elect to receive the remains (the very few parts of loved ones that remained) but instead let the Machine workers dump relatives, lovers, and friends into garbage cans. John (what free parts of him remained) did not belong in the trash. The government had me collect his plastic-bagged body from a local mortician at the back entrance of the Machine factory, later that day. Our friends did not come, for fear that they would be arrested for some arbitrary claim and end up with the same fate. I stood alone with Dr. Emerson. His old eyes did not smile at me, at all. He waited for it to be five o'clock, so he could call his workday over (when he would no longer be surrounded by dead people). When Dr. Emerson looked at me, it was as if he was looking at a dead person, too. I was dead to him. I was as dead as John's Body in that Plastic Bag. My image somehow Died With Him, according to Dr. Emerson. In a way, I was just like what was left of John's corpse. I didn't feel anything. If the Machine guards tried to talk to me, to make eye-contact, I stared into space, unable to linger on the loose strands of their conversation. It was near evening when the bag was finally released. John's body reeked and I was sure that it had started to decay. A mockingbird sang and I felt nauseous. My stomach caved in on itself and started to howl and I felt so bitterly alone, so empty. Suddenly, I wasn't living. I was watching my life on a movie screen (eating popcorn, my feet up on the seats in front of me) and someone just shot a huge hole through the screen. The hole was black and enormous and blocked out everyone's faces. Nothing would be the same, now that John was gone. I would have to rebuild my life around that hole, because nothing would bring him back, not ever. I gagged in the back alleyway. I sobbed and my tears drained my remaining energy to stand. I was on my own, in a strange and empty world that I had to fight on my own. I don't know how I got back to the apartment, but I remember lying on my bed for a long time without realizing where I was. I felt the cool on the pillow next to me. I picked up a strand of his hair. I cried out alone at night in an empty bed, reminiscent of his smell from past mornings, suddenly silent with death.

John's funeral was on a Tuesday. I wish that I could say it was raining or that there were millions of old women crying in the street, but neither occurred. Not even his sister, Joan (or her son William) showed up. It was like I was all the family that John had left in the world. I was the only family that could associate with him after his dreadful death. I imagined that his relatives were too afraid that they would be caught by the quick grasp of the Machine, too. Or, perhaps they didn't want to be identified as the relatives of a fighter, a convict, a deviant from society. They didn't want to be caught supporting his views in public, for fear of public punishment, when secretly they must have agreed with him.

I figured I would never love again. No one would ever touch me. I didn't want to be touched. I would be scum to the Earth. I imagined my body growing old with decay and brittle from the lack of the soft oil of human fingertips. I imagined my carcass melting into sand, skin like an alligator but with holes like Swiss cheese. I would decay just as rapidly as what was left of John's rotting corpse. Invisible bugs and disease would fester in my untouchable remains, my barren cadaver, and my useless body. I wilted away, like a medieval painting under too much light. No. I wasn't the paper crinkling. I was the Self-Portrait. I was Dorian Gray's Portrait (the innocent one, reflecting a nasty image). I was just an effigy, after all. What was I, without the living man?

You must realize that I think (now) that that was a very foolish way for me to look at the world. I still had a life ahead of me, and John would have wanted me to live it. I would be alone, but all I needed was me (my mind and my soul). All I needed was my own memory, which was all I would ever have. When I was little, my mother sent me to Sleep-Away Camp and I became very homesick. I called her up and I told her how much I missed home.

Home, she sternly mumbled through the receiver, is not a place. It's a state of mind. Home will travel with you. You are your own home, your own shelter. All you need is yourself.

I wouldn't be alone, because I had myself to share my own experiences with. All I needed was one body to live through the pain and joys of life. That was all I needed.

John and I never talked about what would happen if one of us ever died (as if it wasn't inevitable). Not to mention if one of us died in our Cause. We never spoke much about each other when we talked about the future. We believed in self-sacrifice at the highest, that (above all) to help other people was our calling. John never really talked much about himself. He never woke up in the morning and thought *I'm in a bad mood today; I don't want to do any work. I'm just going to lie in bed and not doing anything and that'll be fine.* When John wasn't doing his own commissions, he worked as a house painter. And even then, he never complained about making ends meet. He just thought ahead. We never relaxed. We never smiled, unless it was something defiant against this evil cause. We never just blew air onto our foreheads, realizing we had pissed another day away. We never drank beers in our underwear while humming jazz tunes. We never (we never). John was gone. And there were so many things that we hadn't done. We never went on a proper date together (dinner and a movie, the whole deal). We met at a Protest. We never sang Beatles songs, together. Or debated over which side of the bed we liked more. We were never quiet together. We never just sat in our own presence and enjoyed each other's company. We never talked about anything other than Politics. And that was fine (we got a lot of work done for the Rest Of The World). But in the end, I just felt empty and burnt out. I felt like a flesh-eating bacterium was thinning me, sucking away at my bones as I stood looking out at the factory.

I wanted John back. I wanted his soul in his body and I wanted him to talk to me. I wished I could touch his smile once more (the way the lines in his cheeks crinkled when he moved them, when he looked at me and when he liked the feeling of my cool palms around his mouth). Touching his still, chemical-corroded face wasn't the same. It wasn't him at all. I knew what we would talk about: We would talk about the Machine. He would just push me harder to stop its control. But, John would not tell me how to get over him. He would not tell me to do the laundry, even though he was gone. He would not tell me *Stop crying* or *Find someone else*. He would not say that I had stepped in a puddle and that my clothes were slightly wet. No.

That was what my damp tears were for, to remind me that life went on although the one I loved was gone. Hell, the Machine was still running. It never skipped a beat. If anything, it was spreading like the plague.

Through peer pressure, our government forced neighboring international governments to conform to our communal slaughter. The Commodity Of Death became more fashionable than Jeans And A Coke. I became even more indignant as ignorance spread. Barely anyone died of natural causes anymore (most obituaries originally read Death By Machine, before the government created the euphemism Death By Recreation). The government made it seem as though, through death, these people gave rebirth to energy (instead of just feeding our already skyrocketing supply of technology). The Machine served as the end-all, be-all reproduction.

Why Wonder About The Afterlife, When You Could Die Knowing Your Body Would Generate Energy?

Live After-Life Through The Big Sexy.

People even re-defined Be Fruitful And Multiply to mean obeying a life cycle revolving around the Machine. People worshipped the Machine (people craved it as much as the Machine craved them). And as soon as modern life revolved around Big Sexy, people *needed* the Machine as much as it needed them. It seemed like the two were inseparable.

Until you stepped in.

...elevator...

You were working on something a bit different, before I met you.

While sitting in a maroon lobby, the light glazed over your eye balls like frosting on a cupcake. It was just a light bulb on the chandelier in the lobby. No big deal. Some electric machine, reflecting its outer glass. But you thought about that inner yellow luminosity, raw power and energy, spreading across the room in frenetic light beams, attacking everyone's eyes, not just your own. That initial spark stabbed your eyes and left them bleeding streams of yellow across the room. When you finally looked away, it stained your vision with smoky, black stripes. There were holes where that light once captivated your eye. You remembered playing the Light Game when you were a kid. You would sit in the synagogue and stare at the lights on the ceiling and then chase down those black spiders with your eyes, until you had cornered them to the ground, until they would disappear, your eyes suddenly numb from the pain the lights once rendered, as if your body had forgotten the places on which you had set your eyes in the past. You thought of late nights in the car. You would squint your eyes and shred the street lights into X's, like make-shift stars. Or at night when it rained, and a myriad of light beams spewed from those streetlight fixtures into the road, sprinkling the car with beads of brightness. You wanted to be that light so badly. Each road tells a story of a city at night, and you wanted to be the one to make it burn like day. When people asked you how you would like to die, you proudly exclaimed I Want To Explode! Five Thousand Feet In The Air! Millions Of Pieces Of Me! Scattering Across The Sky! And Pouring Down To Earth! One Big Boom! Something Exciting That Gets It Over With, Quick! Oh, How People Would Scream In Terror! Like Judgment Day! Yes, that would be a much better death, you figured, than dying of boredom in this stupid office lobby. You thought about how you would escape in the end. I Want To Be In A Million Places At Once!

You looked over at the mural on the lobby wall. It had a golden taint that made you think of some impoverished, modernist painter during the New Deal, painting on these office walls to show the beauty of industrialization, an ironic contradiction realized too late. Your eyes traced the painted, smiling faces of engineers, car mechanics, and the general halo around metallic machines (true instruments of change). Apparatuses twirling around illuminated faces. And you wondered about how much of that feeling (like a hole in the wall) was just being plastered over so that it seemed fixed without actually being stabilized (like taking a placebo and hoping it will work, like keeping the expensive car and getting another mortgage) was still alive within the people around you, in this office building.

The woman at the main desk, her engine must have been working, you thought. You looked at her type *go go go! Produce! Be productive!* She must have been thinking. What about that man there? Sitting with his arm stretched out over his thigh as he read the newspaper, and his tie dipped below his pants. Hmmm. Looks Like Maladroit Machismo. You diagnosed him right away. Better Take A Look Under The Hood. You thought this whole building was just eating off the energy of the motors within. Was *your* motor feeding this machine? Was it just the painting behind you radiating this work ethic? Or was this workaholic religion emitting from your sweating pores? Was this behavioral? Or genetic? At what point in your life were you taught that you had to be Productive to Accomplish Something (anything) in this world? Remember that whole Be Fruitful gag? You watched that receptionist glow with pride. How she glimmered every Monday morning, how she gleamed to seize the day. Behind that sunbeam of a smile lived a twenty-something caffeine addict, jolting through a catacomb of darkness. Would you enlighten her that day?

You saw some skinny, albino guy go up to the counter. He cocked his hip to one side and you saw something strange protruding from his pocket. You thought he was a eunuch, carrying around his Unmentionables. You watched the woman at the counter give a fake, perky (but really an I-can't-wait-until-it's-five-o'clock) smile to the man with the mysterious pocket package and you wondered if she was used to faking it. You weren't born yesterday. (You weren't born in this office either, so everything seems unfamiliar and strange.) You wondered if she had ever really felt lust, love; the real tingly feeling that fills you more than any cup of coffee or chai. You wondered if there was some reason she hid behind that desktop demeanor. Did she have some secret? Some terrible mauve scar on her thigh that she covered with make up when she secretly went out on Saturday nights, wearing fishnets and a cut jean skirt so short that the pockets hang below the hem? When it started raining, did she run to make sure the scar would not unveil? Was she ashamed when the makeup rubbed off in bed? Would she blush the same color as the scar itself? What did she tell the man in bed next to her before she ripped off his head like a good little praying mantis? Did she date his best friend next?

You sure had some dirty thoughts, if you really think about it.

Across the room, the receptionist saw that you were staring at her. And she lowered her pursed lips together, examining you up and down. She dissected you and then made a final decision.

We'll be ready for you in a minute, the receptionist dismissed you with her eyes, rolling them upward toward the eunuch. She seemed even more tired and bored than when you first noticed her. And you started to wonder when she would collapse in your arms. When would you take her back to your apartment? When would she quit her job to spend all her days with you? She would never quit her job to be with you. Why should she have to? You were not going to convert her to some Anti-Capitalist Movement that would change her perception of materialism forever. She would rather deal with Bureaucratic Bullshit than have to deal with yours. At least bureaucrats had power and some say in this world. She would rather wear a business suit for them, than fancy lingerie for you, though both just hide her scar. Her life was a façade. She was living under a cover. And she was a government spy. A double agent living a double lie.

Ms. Reiner will see you now, the receptionist tilted her head to get you to move. Take the elevator in the hall to the tenth floor. And go to room Ten Forty Three.

Thank you, Miss...

You're welcome. Have a nice day. Her painted-on smile diminished as she turned her head yet again to the eunuch, ignoring that your presence had ever been there; you were only a dimple in the many deep wrinkles of her day (the scarred flesh she would nightly return home to, only to face in the mirror with punctured eyes).

You didn't care. You just rounded the corner and saw the entrance to the stairs (you didn't care that it was ten flights either). You'd feared elevators since you were a kid. You'd always hated all machines. Did you think of the night when you were eight? How it drizzled as you walked into the apartment complex that your mother, Helen, lived in with her new boyfriend, Darryl? Your feet were wet, because when your father dropped you off, you accidentally stepped into a puddle. Your feet tracking water marks, you made your way to the small, cramped elevator inside. In the gush of cold wind from opening the metallic door, your fingertips fluttered down the open cuffed sleeves of your hooded sweater jacket. They could have turned purple any minute. Who knew? You wrapped the unzipped edges around your skinny body (feeling the piercing touch of frozen metal zipper against your soft skin, it was sticking). You wished you didn't have any open orifices, any more. There was music playing, some low volume rhythm, some smooth jazz tune supposed to comfort those returning from a long day at work. You fingered the elevator button. The light shone through your translucent skin. And then as you entered the empty hall (like the stomach of a whale) you saw how the water was still dripping from your parka onto to the floor.

Better watch that, said the security guard to the side. Holding the wet cotton sleeves in your hand, you made your way onto the elevator's conveyer belt. You wanted that machine to help you. Help you make it through this awkward journey from parent to parent. Somehow comfort you. Reassure you in its even lift to the top that things would be alright. That even though the social institution of Family had broken down, this elevator would make it. Yes, this small box of light and music would take you there, to some higher plain. The journey would be alright, even if the end result wasn't. You would have the ride to think all of that over. But on the way up to Mom and Darryl on the fourth floor, the lights went dark, all movement stopped. The only sound other than the wrenching metal was the sound of your shallow breath as you crashed down to the basement. How did you survive? The police didn't know. Surely that ton of metal should have killed you, had you not stood directly under the emergency latch. Never again, you decided. Never trust a machine again.

After the first five flights, you needed a moment to catch your breath. Already the stairs were getting to you. And you sweat through your first layer of expensive, Dry Clean Only clothing. Why, you wondered, was it so expensive just to take care of things that were originally expensive? If they cost more originally, shouldn't they be less costly to take care of? You paused by a small window with blinds looking down to the fire escape and a brick alley. You daydreamed about all of the people who met in that alley (a pregnant drug-dealer looking to sell her body on the side, a mugger and a business man, rapists dragging in their latest victim). Anyone could witness their actions so plainly from this window. No wonder elevators are so shielded from the outside world. They serve more purposes than one. It's easy to see why elevators would be sources of comfort for the people inside. They serve as modern-world wombs. Music, closed space, warmth, censored from the world below, exerting no energy (just being lifted along to a higher plateau). Enough about elevators. You had more important things to do. You were going to force the tenth floor to meet with the ground floor, to meet with the basement. You were going to get someone upstairs, someone with all the power in the world, to meet the needs of the people downstairs (people who desperately needed some attention).

You mounted the next five flights (slower this time) thinking as you made each heavy step. Surely, by now the woman downstairs would get a call from Ms. Reiner asking where her next appointment was. The woman would think that either you'd skipped the meeting or that you had some cataclysmic mental collapse in the elevator, leaving you drooling and paralyzed from the waist down. No, they would just think you were being rude and late, wasting their time because you were an Environmental Freak, taking the stairs instead of the elevator to conserve energy and even to lose some weight. Oh, the fools. If only they knew.

Ninth floor. And finally (yes, you panted) the tenth! You opened the door out of the stairwell into the sanitized hallway of offices. You noticed a shinning porcelain water fountain with a metal handle. You took a sigh of relief and quickly stepped toward it, placing your fingers around the cool handle, and then caressing your lips with the ice water. It froze your throat a little, but you didn't mind, it was so refreshing. You remembered the time in elementary school when kids lined up after gym to use the water fountain. They would try to make you laugh so water would come pouring out of your nose. You wondered where those kids were now. You wondered if any of them made it to this city building.

You turned your head and noticed the office numbers: Ten Ten. Ten Twelve. Then, a large metal plaque *Ten Ten - Ten Thirty, Ten Thirty One - Ten Sixty*. You headed to the right, down another pristine, oh-so-clean office hallway. You saw a Latina cleaning woman heading for a bathroom to the side. You nodded at her, but she kept her eyes toward the cleaning cart, not meeting your glance. She didn't want to talk to someone who would fake two lines of Spanish trying to Meet Her On Her Level. And even if you really did see her as your equal, trying to empathize with her life, connect to her state of being, it wouldn't work.

Continuing to walk, you finally came upon Ten Forty Three with the name plate *Ms. Judith Reiner, State Deputy Commissioner*. You knocked on the door and a warm alto voice greeted you.

Come in, come in.

Judith Reiner (age forty-seven, brown hair, almond brown eyes, five foot six inches tall, two hundred nine pounds), sat in her large leather chair behind a mahogany desk with a big, crescent-moon smile.

Take a seat. And let's go over what you told me over the phone.

You quickly took a seat. You weren't worried about leaving sweat stains on your pants or the chair anymore, as long as you got your message out. You started, Ms. Reiner. I recently quit my job for a computer company. It was a great job. Good pay. Great benefits. But, I found out something horrifically disturbing about company policy. The computer company was creating a new series of games called The Pleasure Package. In the games, the players were given a square viewing set that attached to their faces and projected sounds, images, and smells from the computer. Then, the players were given a

Feeler, a glove that the player could put his hand inside to feel and participate in the game. At first, the series was geared toward children. Educational Material. The children would be in a forest orchard and they would have to pick a certain number of fruits. Then, the product was geared toward adolescents. Mostly violent games. The players could strangle other players. Hear screams. Smell smoke. Chemicals. And even Blood. The game was even advertised through commercials on television, using subliminal messaging. This product sold at a large rate, to the dismay of many parents. Soon however, a new Adult Version came out, where adults could strangle their bosses. Parent's clamor soon died down, as the product became even more popular.

What's your point? Ms. Reiner was getting impatient. We live in a laissez-faire economy. I can't regulate popular products. Especially not Videogames, which aren't physically harmful.

You don't understand. These games *are* harmful. People posted real pictures of their bosses in the game. Real people were being attacked in the game.

Freedom of speech. The game is not *real*.

But then the psychological inhibitions of peoples' consciences were destroyed. After killing their bosses ten times in the game, they couldn't stand walking in to work the next morning with their bosses still alive. They would go to work and actually kill their bosses. In real life. It propagated murders.

In a lawsuit, you wouldn't be able to prove that the game was directly responsible. She started to fiddle with something on her computer. It was the worker in the first place who wanted to kill his boss, remember?

But that wasn't all. Then they came out with this X-rated Pleasure Package. Not only was the gamer given a glove, but also another attachment to the computer. Attached directly to the player's groin. In these games, the players raped and mutilated any one they wanted from reality. I've found that in this tri-city area alone, the rape and murder rate has increased twenty-five percent since the game's release. It's still increasing. I quit my job. I'd had enough. Please, Ms. Reiner. Please. You have to do something about this. You have to stop this product from being sold. You have to stop the use of these machines. You owe it to your people.

Her eyes watched you. Focused more on your accent of each syllable than the words themselves. Oh yes, she's heard it all before. But, she hadn't heard it the way *you* said it. Of course she had already made her decision on the matter, which was final before you ever entered the room, before you even made the phone call. Elections were in a few weeks. And she needed to be on top.

I want to thank you for coming in. You've given this problem plenty of new light. I like your ideas.

But what about *your* ideas? You're the State Commissioner. What are you going to do about it?

First of all, I'm only *Deputy* State Commissioner. At least until the coming fall elections, you see. You will *vote,* I'm sure. She looked down at you and gave a plastic smile before taking a breath and looking up at the ceiling (lying to you, making up the same answer she told to every Joe Shmo with a cause). Second, this is a complicated issue. I have to take this to different committees to discuss and then pass legislation. It will all be drawn out to such unbelievable proportions. Not to mention the cost it will take for the media to garner public recognition of the issue and support. Et cetera. Et cetera. Not a problem that can be solved with easy answers.

But don't you have *any* answers? How are you going to handle this?

Ms. Reiner's fat fingers massaged her temples. She'd had enough of this guy with a conscience who thought he could change the world. She was tired and the caffeine headache started to kick in. I think we're done for today. Thank you for stopping by and voicing your opinion.

But you didn't...

I will make a note of it. And please don't forget to vote in the upcoming election.

I don't think you...

Thank you for stopping by, she said. Concluding your relationship with the stare in her eyes. Have a nice day.

...make a friend...

You walked out of the office building onto the busy streets below. You realized this time the bureaucrats really didn't care if someone was raped or murdered. Ms. Reiner didn't care about her constituents as long as they voted. She didn't care what their mental or physical shape was. Most of all, she didn't care about their morals. She didn't care if they raped or killed each other, as long as at the end of the day, she was still in charge.

You just stood there a minute, by the side of the street, mouth open. You were in shock and disgust at the people upstairs. You didn't care if they were looking down anymore. Fuck them. You stared down their linoleum mentality, their sheet metal windows, and how their buildings artificially reflecting the sun. For a second there, you wished their offices converged with the sun (melting office ware, exploding pencil holders, metal filling cabinets bursting into flames, trapping people inside their beige prison). The smell of rotting flesh flirted with your nostrils. No. No, you wouldn't let it get to you, you wouldn't let them drag you down with the rest (you wouldn't stoop to their level). You knew the power of the mind. You knew its freedom to contain thoughts prohibited in action. But you also knew that in this Modern American Society, thought always translated to action. There was no middle ground of Security or Privacy. The government took care of that with their wire taps and spying. The media enforced it with ads like *What Have You Got To Hide?* The American Dream turned thoughts into realities, to the benefit or deterioration of the people.

While standing there, you realized that the deviants in this world were intellectuals with morals, considered anarchists, those resisting the oppressive state. Just when you thought things couldn't get worse; a religious group came over to proselytize you. Two miniature, dark-haired women and a forty-year-old, tanned man crowded around you, handing you two blue pamphlets. The first said *Recognize The Ruler* and the second *Make A Friend.* Because things couldn't get worse, right? Their smiling faces struggled desperately to entice you as they shoved their booklets in your face. They weren't the usual Jesus freaks that you saw on Sundays. No. No, these people were in a class of their own.

We come from the Planetary Alliance, the man told you. We want to bring you home.

Oh God, you thought, they're delusional conversion freaks! Some sci-fi cult comes to claim me, wrap their claws around me and chew my head off. Shoot me now.

What are you? one of the girls asked.

What am I? you asked back.

Yeah. You know? Christian, Jew, Muslim? she explained. What are you?

You shrugged your shoulders, not understanding why anyone on the street would directly ask you that question, unless they were about to pounce.

They were fed up with your lack of response. They wanted you to give a firm response. Because they were trained to break it down for you. It didn't really matter what you were to them, as long as you had some sort of strong motivation behind it.

You believe in *The One*, don't you?

You shook your head at them and looked down at your shoes. You just weren't in the mood to fight the devil today, to fight fire with fire, not after what you'd been through.

Right now, I'm not sure I believe in anything, you said bleakly. And their mouths closed around you.

A nihilist, they figured. And a pessimist, at that. No hope there.

They spotted a group of teenagers crossing the street and walked away. You wondered where their charismatic founder was. Was he bathing in a gold shower? Was he sleeping with two of his child-lovers? Where were their parents during this debauchery? Where was the founder's soul?

You felt the chill of autumn and grabbed the sides of your coat, pulling them closer toward you, imagining the edges of the cloth as arms wrapping around your chest. It was getting cold. It was only mid-October. You wondered about what to do with the remainder of your wasted day. You decided just to go home. So you walked the three blocks to the bus stop and you got on, not caring about how bad traffic would be at this hour.

Well, the traffic was pretty bad. The cars trapped the bus into the far right lane of a three-lane, one-way road. After twenty five minutes of waiting to pull back into traffic at a corner, you wondered if you made the right decision. I just want to get home, you thought. And so you waited as the bus driver sifted through the sea of machines. Finally, your stop came up. And you walked the five blocks to your apartment complex.

The evergreen trees in front of the building started to turn blood red and skin yellow. Leaves fell like an open wound, oozing into the street. There was a large, rented white moving truck unloading packages and you shook your head, not ready for new neighbors, today. You couldn't be cordial today. Not with another unsuspecting victim of corporate takeover. Machine takeover. You tossed your head back in the wind, as if desperately trying to brush off your broken heart, your loss of faith in humanity. What could you do? You had a bad day.

A fat head of dark red hair appeared from behind the front door and you recognized it right away as Sarah McKinney's. Sarah (age thirty-nine) lived in the apartment below you. She had two small, red haired children, Mary (age five) and Pete (age nine) and lived with her tall, brunette husband, Matt (age forty-one). Sarah worked for the local gazette as a news reporter. Matt worked as a manager for a local television studio.

I'm so glad you're back! She spotted you, motioning for you to enter the room. We have a new neighbor. This is...

Do you remember first meeting me? I remember you looked very tired and a little upset. I was lifting a box of books when you first saw me. My hair was a mess and I was really sweaty from unloading. You didn't say much to me. You just said something like Nice to meet you. And then you went upstairs and shut your door. I didn't see you until the next morning, when I was still awake from unpacking.

The next afternoon, Sarah stood in the hallway helping me get rid of the old boxes. Hey! Come 'ere and get to know your new neighbor, she told you (like a mother would). You walked closer and saw my open door. Peering inside to see that I had a ways to go. You decided to make conversation. You asked me where I had moved from. I told you Not far from here. Near the factories. By the shore. Someplace a little nicer than this.

Then why did you move?

Do you remember how my eyes glared upon the question? Do you remember me stopping, mouth open, as if you didn't know (how could anyone be so oblivious to the pain and suffering our people were now experiencing). But instead of rushing into a political frenzy, I took my time. I said plainly, as if monitoring your reaction They built a Machine Factory next to my building.

A Machine Factory? you said. Well, there are plenty of those down there. Wouldn't you already be used to that? It's not like they forced you out of your home, was it?

It wasn't the type of Machine I could get used to, I replied. It was one of those Killing Machines.

Oh! entered Sarah in the conversation. You mean one of those Energy Machines!

Don't be silly, you said to her response. They're Death Machines. More and more today, all machines are becoming Death Machines.

I think I fell in love with you right at that moment.

Gosh, don't put it like that, Sarah said. You make it so depressing. People are consciously aware of what they're doing. They're helping the community.

Don't be so oblivious, I said.

And then you looked at me. Happy with my tone. And looked back at Sarah saying, Don't you have a conscience?

Pete came running up the stairs to find his mother with a crooked look on her face. Matt followed, carrying Mary in his arms. Ugh, he said, heaving her down onto the concrete. What a long day. He kissed his wife. How was your day, honey?

Sarah stood there stationary, still trying to wipe off your last remarks. She shook her head and blinked her eyes a little. Fine, dear. Just fine.

She looked down at Mary (her nose was dripping and Pete gave her a big hug).

Mommy!

And how was your day, sweetie?

It was okay!

Did you miss your Mommy?

Mmm hmm, he said, looking up at me, questioning my unfamiliar face.

Pete, this is our new neighbor, introduced Sarah.

Hi Pete, I said, waving a hand toward his small face. Pete grabbed his mother's leg and held tight, hiding behind it. He was shy around new people.

Aw Pete, said Sarah, trying to encourage him to be friendly. Oh, well. I should go help make dinner. Is there anything else that you need? You have my number in case of an emergency.

Yes. Thank you so much, Sarah.

No problem, she answered.

Maybe I should give you mine too, you blurted out. Just in case of an emergency.

Okay, I said. As you told me the numbers one by one, I dialed them into my cell phone, imagining your lips curled around each syllable. Thanks, I replied at the end. Maybe I could call you some time. For dinner or something. I don't know a lot about what's around here.

Sure, you said, knowing that the shore wasn't that far away to make things unfamiliar. Sure.

…were you still worried?…

I called you on a Thursday night. It was raining and I unplugged the TV because I didn't want to watch commercials anymore. You answered the phone like you had just woken up. It wasn't that late, but your throat churned a little. Maybe you'd been crying. I'm not sure. Was something upsetting you, at the time? Were you still worried about your job? I asked if you wanted to go to a rally with me. You cleared your throat at my forward gesture and said I didn't know you were that political.

There are a lot of things about me you don't know (I thought in my head *But I want you to find out*).

What kind of rally?

Well, I know we only talked for a moment about the Machine, but it's an Anti-Death Rally. It's taking place on the beach. We could catch a bus and go down there. It would be nice.

You know I tried to do something, a little while ago. To fight the political-mechanical entanglements in our society. It didn't really work.

I paused for a moment. You were very serious. I was serious, too. But I was an Optimist. It's only a protest. What will it hurt you to attend?

Alright, you said. What time should I meet you?

…massacre, in brief…

The beach was salty.

We arrived. And when we saw the hundreds of cars parked along the highway, we got excited. When we saw the hundreds of police cars that followed, our spirits diminished. The leaders of the protest started moving slowly, banners and megaphones in hand. They dominated the cliffs overlooking the ocean. We were screaming for Freedom and for Life, singing songs, calling for an End To The Slaughter. Little did we know the massacre was about to begin.

It started with William B. Erenow, a teenager with manic depression from Brooklyn who was staying with his aunt and cousin for the weekend. The police started to come closer and closer to the protestors as we gathered along the edges of the cliff. The sun started setting. William got scared. Were you? I worried sometimes when we were there, did you? Looking at all those men with sticks and helmets? William threw the first stone at the policemen as they charged toward us. People watched as the violent ones escaped by jumping over officers. The nonviolent protesters were slowly pushed nearer and nearer to the edge of the cliff. How silent it was, when the fighting first erupted! As if the whole world were watching as the last pacifists were slaughtered by the most powerful Democratic Nation in the world. People started to spill over the edge of the cliff, as the police pressed us further and further toward the crust of the land. There wasn't enough room for all of us. Then the screaming. You're Killing Us! You Nazis! screamed an older man. Stop! But the police kept driving and driving the people into the sea, as if we weren't even worthy of the Machine, as if our bodies weren't good enough to be converted into energy. We just needed to die and to have our souls dispersed randomly in the universe.

More and more people started falling over the cliff. The back row was gone over the side, their voices muted by the crashing shore, the rocky cliffs ripping open their bodies along the side. More and more sirens kept ringing, as the police mounted and mounted, with greater speed and force, pushing the people down the sides. Die Damn You! one of them screamed out like an order. Three...Two...One... the Captains kept yelling out to the others, as if this destruction was somehow ordered and civilized. Whatever it was, it was still murder. We were pushed closer and closer to the back, when suddenly the row behind us started to slip, falling under, grabbing the tips of the cliff, only to have their knuckles stepped on by the next row of protestors. One man's bone was exposed in his bleeding hand as he held on for dear life and screamed out to heaven. Oh God! Save Me! He fell moments later. Impaled on a tree root that stuck out from the side.

I tripped then (do you remember?). I fell back on top of the other bodies below. There must have been at least ten that I lay on top of, half of them dying. And then you fell, too. Only to meet me at the bottom of the hill of bodies, as we both rolled down, crushing others. I tried to get up, after a moment of lying on my stomach on the ground, blacked out from the hard three-story roll. I raised my chest, but I could not breathe. And I fell back down, again. My face planted in the sand. I felt like my bones crushed my lungs. I started to cough and gag and I ate the bloody sand to stop myself. Do you know what I saw when I passed out? I saw the ghosts of the people around me, gathering around my live body, jealous of my ability to gain revenge. I remember that you called out to me from far away. I could hear you in the darkness. I didn't mean for any of this to happen (but we had to speak out against the Machinocide). We still had to be together as a community to fight this, didn't we? (I imagine that you thought a few individuals might have had more weight than a group that could easily be pushed off a cliff). When I opened my eyes, I heard heavy breathing from my lungs and the people around me. Are you alright? some man called out. I could see again. I wished I couldn't. I saw the debris around me, dead bodies, some alive, some crawling along the sides of the cliffs, praying for some safe ground. It should have been in black and white, some war documentary about the carnage of a battle. I wish it hadn't been in color. Blood, dirt, and wet sand scattered everywhere. A woman to the right literally fell into the rocky sea, drowning in her bruised and bashed in skin, sore from the salt and sand that sucked her dry. I remembered praying for her. Did you pray for the rest of us?

The police finally backed away, arresting twenty people (taking them away in their big trucks) and leaving the rest of us for the ambulances. A lot of people got up and ran away. Those who could no longer walk were rounded up by ambulances and driven away. And then it was just you and me. Alone on the shore. Gaping blindly at the abyss in front of us. The sun setting only to create a gigantic black hole in the sky behind us.

I decided to sit on the sand (the wet grains splattered all along my jeans) just so I could rest. You didn't notice, at first. You were too distracted by how quickly the sand absorbed the blood on the ground. But then your eyes began to wander past the nausea. You saw me sitting there, arms crossed, head in my knees, seeking refuge from the unmerciful sun. The water was glistening. I'm tired, I spoke finally. And you sat down next to me, in disbelief that I could talk after such an event had taken place, and that those were my choice of words.

I'm sick and tired of fighting this. It's over our heads, you said.

No. Don't you understand? I looked up at you, my eyes soft with tears. I'm tired of the violence. I'm tired of the fact that everything in this country leads to death. I'm tired of the constant turmoil. Why can't we make it better? Why can't we fill the void? I started rambling. And a tear dropped down my frowning chin. I wiped the tear from my face. I'm sorry. I...

You held my hand. It's okay. It's going to be alright.

...living in eternal summer...

We didn't go back to the apartment complex, just then. Instead, we stayed on the shore for awhile, talking.

When I was little, you said to me, I always thought that things were perfect. Being innocent is like living in heaven.

It's like living in eternal summer, I agreed. All I can remember from when I was little was running around in my backyard, in the sunshine. And then I grew up and I realized that there were the same problems in politics and poverty back then as now. It just took me a while to comprehend it. I realized that there were impoverished migrant workers chopping and cutting morning grass in that backyard that I loved so much. I realized that the neighbors didn't like the gardeners because they were Mexican. I find out that my neighbors tried to get them deported, but failed. Because they *were* citizens. And then I realized that the machinery was ingrained in our society, from the beginning. That the pain was harvested for years. And that the latest Machine is only an accumulation of the years and history of Machinocide, beforehand. This isn't new. It was bound to happen, at some point. The government was going to come out with this, just like the Atomic Bomb. How is an Atomic Bomb any different than the Machine? People knew just as much after those first explosions as they know now. And they're fine with it.

You sighed for a minute and then asked Where were you when you first heard about the machine?

Well, I heard about the *Corporations,* first. I heard they were trying to buy A Machine. And I doubted that it would sell. But, I was wrong. Human greed for money is stronger than compassion or insatiability for life. As long as some corporate junkie's life is sophisticated and comfortable with his many gadgets, what does he care if there are thousands being killed on the street? *Quality* of life is what they care about, not *Quantity*. I paused. I wasn't answering your question, I was just blubbering my own political rhetoric. When the government first announced, or rather Advertised, this new Cost Effective Energy Solution I was a senior in high school. The loudspeaker went on in school. And we were told to turn on the television. We watched in awe as beautiful colors advertised the Machine for the first time. On CNN. My teachers observed with horror and disgust. And then *awe*. When I came home from school, watching TV at the dinner table, the same commercials came on. The same government style, with a little more flavor for the slaughter. Recorders of history won't even be able to quantify it into genocide, because they're after everyone, not just certain groups.

I was angry, the blood rushed to my face and a chilly wind blew sand against my skin. I pulled my coat closer toward my throat and asked you When did you first hear?

Around the same time. I called it Black Tuesday. The day when the government first came out with those commercials. I was working on statistics homework when my friend Mike Tailor called and told me to turn on the TV. He said it sounded great. He was an environmental freak and all that. I'm not sure that I understood what it meant, at first. I don't think anyone could fully comprehend it. Maybe if there was someone who detached herself from the propaganda, from its effects, maybe she knew the effects these commercials would produce. I remember I sat down. Stared blindly at my homework. And then started to use my small knowledge of statistics to figure out my chances of survival. It was so natural. I did it without thinking. One Million Killed In This Area...Another Million Here... All Volunteers. Could you believe that these people *wanted* to die?

No. And I still can't, I told you honestly.

Maybe I can. Maybe because they were so addicted to machines already. They couldn't see life without any. But still...

I know. The facts sat in a pit at the bottom of my stomach. Did you cry? I remember crying when I found out what they were really advertising.

I cried when my friend, Susan Doughtry's mother died in the Machine. And when the government came out with the numbers. The number of people that were volunteering. They came in droves! Oh, the government was so proud of all their followers.

...maybe we need followers...

What? You looked confused.

Well, if we're going to fight this. I looked at you. Together, that is. Maybe we ought to get some followers. We just need a small trickle of water to crack the dam. We should show people that the Machine is wrong. You shook your head as if it was impossible. Look, I stared in your eyes. I'm not giving up. If the majority of people knew that this was an unjust system, if they knew the repercussions of what they are doing to mankind, and they knew that they could choose an alternative, then things would change. If we took the government's followers out from under them, then we could bring about a social revolution.

Such a preacher, you said, tossing your head in the air.

I tried to fight this thing, before. And I'm willing to try again. Are you with me or not? You were silent and I stared right at you. If you don't do anything to stop the government, you're just as bad as they are. If you don't join me, you might as well join the volunteers waiting around the corners of abattoirs like flocks of sheep, blindly following their Shepherd, waiting for the slaughter. A troop of soldiers waiting for their final orders to join the carnage. A herd of cows heading to McDonald's. Pigs waiting for the butcher's knife! My voice started getting louder and louder and you got up and started to walk away. I got up and followed you. Why are you silencing yourself before the government even has a chance to take your voice away from you? Speak! Speak out!

I tried! you yelled and faced me. I tried for a smaller problem at a higher level. And nothing happened! Don't you understand that it didn't work? We can't win!

I grabbed your cool cheeks and looked straight into your eyes. We sure as hell can! Or else we're going to end up with the same horde of people. Waiting to die.

...romantic, if anything...

Come get some food with me. The words rolled off your tongue so naturally I would have thought that they'd been growing there for years, or that you'd planted those syllables there only to pluck them out for certain girls.

What? (It's difficult to think of food when the world is ending).

Come get some food with me. Go out with me. You took my hand, again. And held it. The lights were out all over the beach. And the hobos started to wander the shoreline. I want to do this together.

I guess... I just need to get to know you better.

How could I trust you then? Do you understand why I stalled? You might have just been manipulating me. A good lay at the end of the day. I just didn't know if you would change sides on me suddenly (if you would support me until the very end).

So, go out with me. And you can get to know me better. You started bumbling around your footsteps, nagging and whining gently (playfully) to the point where pity curved my lips into a smile.

Ok. Alright.

It was difficult for me to go on a date when the world was ending. It wasn't for you. You found it more exciting (Romantic, if anything) that two Saviors Of The World would take a break from fighting to restore their energy. I didn't understand your comfort and excitement, just as I didn't understand how people could make dead baby jokes (or laugh at all, for that matter) when they discuss times of turmoil and crisis. You told me that during Jewish holidays you had always been taught that the major theme was First They Tried To Kill Us, They Didn't, Let's Eat! You told me that the greatest jokes were based on turmoil. And without turmoil, you told me no one could laugh. Was that like claiming that without Bad there is no Good? Or without Sadness, no Happiness? Perhaps we just lived in a limbo land, a world between heaven and hell, where good and evil met on an even playing field. But then why fight things at all? If only to restore the natural balance once again? Why take the world from a negative score only to reach the zero it started at? Why couldn't this end positively?

We walked to a nearby shore front restaurant called The Big Fish and we sat there for a moment, escaping from what we knew was necessary. It was more like taking a break, a moment of reflection, feeding our bodies before we fought with all our might the ultimate cause (To Save Humanity). You got swordfish and I got crab cakes. We sat submerged in a thick garlic aroma, drenched in a buttery musk. This was our first date, if you don't include the massacre. This was our first conventional night out together. We'd have this to base the rest of our relationship on. We still needed to create a relationship. We still needed to connect.

At first, you slowly picked at the fish, staring (half smiling) into my eyes, as if this was some great story to tell our kids one day. I was still getting over the fact that there might not be any children in the future. Then you chomped away at a thick piece of fish like a hungry wolf. I'm starving, you said. Rioting made you hungry. I, on the other hand, barely touched my food. And then seeing that you were finishing quickly, I tried to pick at it, my stomach still in knots.

You know I tried this before, I told you. Dating someone who was trying to fight for a cause.

Oh yeah? you said, half caring, the fish stuck in your teeth as you munched away. How long did that last?

Not very long, I commented. And you continued gobbling. He was killed. He was convicted of a nonsense crime and sentenced to Death By Machine. You paused for a moment, a piece of spinach was caught in your teeth. You knew I was being serious. You knew that I had lost someone dear to me in the past and I wasn't quite ready to get attached to someone else I might lose in the future. You also knew that this was the first time you were trying to get to know me, and you had already had your somber fill for the day. He was a painter, I said. Tears started to fill my eyes. He painted posters. Advocating against the Machine.

You know, the number one thing you're not supposed to do on a date is talk about ex-boyfriends, you said slyly, as if you wanted me to get over it. You wanted me to have thicker skin. Especially if I was fighting something with no heart or spine. I chuckled a little. And you said See! There's a smile! I knew it was possible.

Sorry, I replied, blushing.

It's ok, you said. You just have to turn off the water works, once in a while. That's all. Or else you'll never survive. How can anyone survive being so serious all the time? Jesus! You must have had some playmates in school! How could they stand you?

I blushed, again. And you grabbed the waiter. Get this girl ten CCs of laughter! Stat! I started laughing at your outgoing ridiculousness, your extroverted waves of your hands as you began to talk and explain things, like you were performing (like a puppeteer with puppets). You told me jokes and silly anecdotes about School Politics and Running For Senior Class President. You told me stories about how you Overcame Failure.

They got to me, all the time, you told me. About your classmates in high school. They used to do terrible things. Like tease me. And ditch me in strange parking lots, after parties. It wasn't that I didn't feel anything. It was that I felt something greater when I could laugh about it, in the end. All laughter comes out of sorrow. I can swear to that.

We split the check. Revolutionaries can't be conventional. As we walked toward the bus stop, you walked with your hands in your pockets and I put my arm around your arm. I think you're wonderful, I told you.

You're not bad yourself, you said back. Don't worry. Everything is going to work out.

It doesn't seem like it, sometimes, I said. We stopped

walking, under the street lamp above the bus stop. Our shadows gathered like one gigantic blob on the shack where a few others waited for the bus.

But, you're an Optimist, you said. So this has to end well. Doesn't it?

But, are you an Optimist?

Of course I am. I'll prove it to you! And in the dim light, you squeezed my body tight and softly kissed my lips.

...not return to earth...

You rolled over in bed, in the morning. The green globs of dream residue still sticking to your eyelashes. I have one now, you told me. I have another solution.

I turned on the lamp and sat up in bed next to you, arching my back against my pillow toward you to see you better. Your pupils adjusted to the light.

This time, you told me about getting a loan for a big sum. Billions of dollars. From a Bank. From a Drug Cartel. From any place that would give us money. We would use this money to buy a trip in a Russian space shuttle (like they do for all those Trillionaires) to train us to go into outer space. In our little space shuttle, we would lift off and leave the destructive world below, escaping from the carnage of our realities. We would look up to the sky, the shimmering lights all around us, the blue burning inferno below, and finally feel like we were free from the constraints of our society. You held my hand and whispered to me, spurting small spits of excitement. And then, you said, as our Captain tells us that we are soon going to descend back to earth, we will Hijack The Shuttle! Your body quivered with excitement. It oozed from the blisters on your feet and the pores on your face. We will *Not* return to Earth. We will stay in orbit. Forever. Even after our oxygen level runs out and our suffocated purple bodies float without gravity. We will not be grave, at all. We will be sublimely happy. Not dying in the hell below us, but purposely placing ourselves in heaven.

I squeezed your hands and bit your lower lip. Eh! Nice try. Thanks for playing. You kicked my shins. And I told you Try Again. Your dark eyelashes still cluttered with packets of reverie. I wanted you to Save The World. To come up with an answer (with a million answers). I stared into the blank response in your eyes (you must have known, I had always demanded at least that of you). Your face turned blank and pale, your palms were sweating. Plans are all well and good. But it's hard to solve the biggest problem in the world, I said to you. What if we can't do it? What if this one can't have a happy ending?

It will, you told me. It has to.

The second solution that you came up with was to create our own Communities. Communes. Kibbutzim. We could raise our children, there. And educate them.

Children? I asked you. And an empty pit expanded over my ovaries. I should have told you. I should have told you during those first nights of passion, when you started to talk about the future so much. I should have told you how during an abortion the doctors found malignant tissue. I should have told you that it ran in the family. How it was only a matter of time. And that they removed my womanhood, there and then on the operating table.

Fine, you told me. The tears filling our eyes. We'll take other children. We'll take other adults. And we'll Reeducate them.

We had to learn that people are too ignorant to be taught.

Mark Faer was a real estate agent with one gold tooth crookedly hanging on the roof of his mouth. Whenever he smiled the gold would twinkle. I support you. I believe in your cause. You know, I find great comfort in families like yours for the future, he told us.

Oh... I tried to correct him. We're not...

It's people like you that make a good name for your generation.

Um... thank you, you answered.

Now, lets look at the big lots I have opened near the beautiful, rustic, secluded areas of this country. Get you out of the city. This one is outside of Toledo. It's in a place called New Foley. New lands. Open for development. This is one in Carter's Back. And here...

Can we talk about price range for a moment? you asked.

Why sure, he answered, his tooth glimmering in the light, like the sweat on his forehead. Which ones were you interested in?

How much is New Foley?

Now, New Foley is a pricey one. I mean, it would be up there on the price range. About one million. Per acre.

What? The number choked my throat.

Carter's Back is five hundred thousand. Per acre.

Haven't you got anything cheaper? I thought of my meager

earnings, my lack of funds to support such an endeavor. I didn't want to make this into some type of cult, where we made people pay and give us all of their material possessions in order to Live With Us and to Learn What Was Moral And Righteous In This World. How much would it cost to make people survive? How much for a human head? For a life saved from oppression and death? Why were we exiling ourselves from a democratic society?

Willing Grove is the cheapest I got. It's two hundred thousand. Per acre.

We'll think about that, you said. And I stared at you. Silently.

...soon, won't that be nice?...

Move me and my children *where?* Sarah McKinney folded her arms across her chest while leaning against the doorposts adjacent to the hallway, her large body protruding like a raisin in cornflake cereal. She was tired. All day, she'd been trying to fill out inventory slips, walking around and around the building to mark off needed supplies. And the kids had been nagging her in the apartment, staying home from school because they were sick. The bags under her eyes jutted out, like landing decks on an aircraft carrier, her nose as red as a maraschino cherry. She was starting to get sick, too.

Willing Grove is a piece of land. Only twelve miles from here. We could buy it. And build on it.

You showed her a shiny green brochure (something Mark Faer sent you by mail, to add a personal touch of communication with customers).

We're not asking you to do anything truly unorthodox. Look at it like a Kibbutz. Or a Commune. For heaven's sake, take Walden for example...

You've got to be kidding me. Her hands flew up in the air, as if to ask God what she had done to deserve two boarders like this. Look. I'm against this Death Machine, as much as the next mother. But frankly, some liberalized farm without any clean food or water is no place for me. Not to mention, I've been hearing that the government is going to cut down on its spending. Soon, it will only use the Machine for convicts and euthanasia cases. Now, won't that be nice?

...wanna cum, honey?...

The next solution you came up with hit you as we walked to a protest, outside one of the factories. As Sarah McKinney prepared brown paper bag lunches and sent Pete and Mary off to school in the morning, we trudged off to go meet our fate. The night before it had rained and the ground was still damp. Volunteers and prisoners waddled along, waiting outside the building in the puddles. They didn't care that their socks were muddy. This was the end. They thought they were in for the ride of their lives. Only a few stuck out in my mind, in particular. No one usually came dressed for the Machine in their finest attire. Instead, they wore their work clothes, their tired, end-of-the-week pajamas (or just some lingerie). Anything to make them more comfortable. Anything to make the experience more pleasurable. Some faces were expressionless, while others bit their lips in anticipation. Some stationary bodies, some peeing in their pants. Some numb, some shaking in eagerness.

We waved bright red signs reading *Stop Suicide! Stop The Machine!* and *Death Isn't Sexy!* But really, we needed to tell them that Power Wasn't Sexy. Making you more powerful by hurting others wasn't an aphrodisiac. Giving in to power wouldn't make you any more powerful.

I watched as a fat man at the end of the line jacked off underneath his rain coat. A group of eighteen-year-old, tattooed Goths drenched in rain licked each other as they shivered in excitement, like they were preparing for some ultimate rollercoaster ride. They threw a pack of cigarettes in a puddle on the street. It splashed near me. It was as if they were saying Take These To Survive. We Won't Need Them, Anymore. Now, We're Going To Die, Directly. We Don't Need To Beat Around The Bush.

A girl in a trench coat came up to you, as you held your sign. She put her arms around your neck and let her coat slowly, subconsciously, unravel around her hips. Hey, baby. You looking for a good time? Some prostitute, you figured. Some nymphomaniac looking to make a buck before she thinks she goes to heaven (or to hell, you weren't sure).

Fuck off, you told her. And she turned around. And then looked straight back at you and winked, saying, I sure will, baby. It made you sick. She went back to the line and stayed there. Smiling back at you. You wanna *Cum*, honey? You wanna *Watch*? It'll be fun!

Your face was bright red. And you felt the heat of hell festering, blistering your skin. You stomped the puddles with calculated force to make the perfect splash ratio. When you approached me, I saw how the rain dripped down your nose. And I stared at your heated face (red eyes, frowning mouth, scrunched forehead and nose). The lines on your face outlined a map of lies and misconceptions about mankind. You were angry. You pulled me to the side and said, Let's just kill them all! I'm so sick of this! We can't educate them. Let's just cut their resources to the max.

We'll only be killing ourselves. We'll only be helping Man kill himself. It was difficult to think of greater solutions when smaller problems were still biting us in the face. In the midst of our disgust at mankind, you came up with another answer.

You thought that once the Machine was put back solely in the hands of Corporations, our government (and governments around the world) would have no choice but to attack the Corporations for their malevolent, deadly behavior (because the governments themselves weren't receiving any of the profits or benefits and couldn't compete). There was no way of defeating the government, you figured. But, there were ways to defeat Corporations.

...we don't want to own that...

The Business Executives arrived at the meeting, late. The clock on the wall ticked over and over again, its hands parading around the bold numbers like a Cooch Dancer at a Carnival. The maroon desks lay bare and shined against the light revealed from the Japanese blinds on the office room windows. We rented this Conference Room at the Windsor Hotel so that there would be an even playing field, so many Corporations could come to compete, together. We stood at the front of the room, our PowerPoint Projector at the back, staring us down, waiting to punch out artificial light. We made all the cute Corporate Diagrams, Charts, and Graphics to catch their eyes and get them interested in the idea. Their greedy paws wouldn't be able to keep off this hot commodity, we thought.

Slowly, the men and women in pressed black and pressed blue business suits poured into the room, their five hundred dollar coats packed on to the backs of the swivel chairs like the furs of tribal leaders (or the Coats Of Arms of Royalty). The blinds were closed. The windows blackened. And soon we created a new light. The Projector was up and running.

Slide, I said. And you hit the Enter key on the computer.

Globalization, my friends, is a familiar game. This is a Democratic Country. One that believes in Free Trade and Free Opportunity. Why should the government have all the fun? Why should the government monopolize the acquisition of Energy in one giant area? Let's just face it: Corporations are better at regulating Energy around the globe than governments. Corporations have to take back what was originally theirs. Put *Power* back into the hands of the people. *That's* the American dream.

Excuse me, a black, female Executive raised her hand. That slide says *Privatization Of Machine Industries*. Are you proposing that Private Corporations take the Machine's capabilities back into their own hands?

I am. I looked back at you. Now they were starting to get it. Slide. I'm talking Smaller Scale Production, at first. Pet Machines. Plant Machines. And then Home Abortion Kits. The government couldn't claim you were taking their patent if you created a New Idea that has the same capabilities but barely resembles the mass extermination of current Machinery Factory settings.

What about the *Fiscal Effects*? clamored a man in the back of the room, with white hair, wearing a dark bowtie.

Go to slide Eleven... I looked back at you nervously. As you can see, Private Corporations would reap the financial benefits. Aren't Individual Interests more important than the Collective Good? In the Past, your Corporations haven't cared about a National Health Care Coverage System or Educational and Economic Equality to even the playing field for the impoverished. Not to mention the number of PAC's you've donated to, to lobby for Tax Reductions only for the rich, increasing the Upper and Lower Class Gap...

Corporations owning this type of Technology instead of the government? That would *increase* taxes on companies in a minute, a small man who had placed papers from his brief case all over the desk coughed out in disgust. His sarcastic laugh offended me. We would be *decreasing* Company Revenue and *benefiting* the government. As a taxpayer, I'm not willing to do that.

A Chinese Foreign Investor in the back popped up his head. As a Foreign Investor, I'm not willing to, either. The government would shut us down. Or *absorb* us. It would only be a matter of *minutes.*

Not to mention the Moral Implications. A man in the front (with glasses that reflected the projected light) looked over at me, in his blue tie. How could you sum this up in a Code Of Social Responsibility?

Well. The government did a pretty good job of convincing the people that it was the *Right Thing To Do*, you said from the back.

The man in the back looked at you and shook his head. Our Corporations don't want blood on our hands.

But you don't care if it's the government's responsibility? I asked, You would rather leave it up to them?

Leave it up to the people in *Power*, a woman with a long name on a name tag, in tight red shoes, clamored from the back.

But you are the ones that are gaining *More Power* than any government in the entire world. You represent the largest Computer Software Corporations, the largest Fast Food Industries…

People started to gather their things and shuffle out of the room. They shook hands, said farewells and *Hope to see you at a better conference, some time* and *Here's my card.*

I continued, Your Profits control National Economies. You own the Land, the People…

But we don't want to own *This*, said the black, female Executive who had originally interrupted my presentation. And then the lights went on. And the rest of the Executives left. It was over in a flash. Like the wind that rocks your head in a rollercoaster, or the speed that knocks you back while waiting for the subway car door to stop right in front of you. The meeting had come and gone. It didn't work. Corporate Sponsorship wasn't the answer.

…awkward date gone wrong…

I remember standing in that empty Board Room for a long time. I don't remember exactly what I was thinking or feeling. Perhaps I was just numb, for a moment in time. I do remember that you sat down on a chair, head bent toward the floor. You put your hands over your face and sighed a moment, like you had just finished building a gigantic dam all on your own (that took you years to design and finally put into reality) and now watched it crack and break, in an hour. I wondered if you were really feeling the pain that I was. Or if it was just for some sort of show. But you were truly upset. This struck you much harder than the government meeting with Ms. Reiner. And you felt as if you had truly, truly failed. Twice. You wondered if you had kept making the same mistakes over and over again, like some mental patient continually hitting a Shock Button that he was told not to press. You wondered if there was anything that you could have done in the Past to make things different. Maybe if you had majored in Communications or Psychology, you thought, then maybe you could have been more convincing, you could have sold it to them like an Advertisement. But no. That wasn't you. It was them. It was the Executives (sitting in these fancy leather chairs) that just didn't give a damn about anyone's ego, other than their own. At that point, you looked up to me and you knew that it wasn't your fault. You couldn't change their minds. It was Society's problem. I wish I had known what you were thinking. Because although I would have agreed that Society did play a large role in making everyone a little more egocentric, it was still our responsibility to do something about it.

You got up from the chair and you held my hand for a moment. Aw, don't get so down, you said smiling at me. Better luck next time. And you kissed my cheek, grabbed your coat, and walked swiftly out of the room. I'll call you, you said (as if this was some sort of awkward Date Gone Wrong and you wanted a do-over). I was upset, at first. But your empathy slightly cheered me up. I left the room and I blushed a little, holding my cheek in the palm of my hand.

On the way back to my apartment, I ran into Sarah (who was doing a Heating Check). Her small, round body quickly jiggled back and forth like a quail on the way to feed her children. She scurried from room to room, making little notes on a clipboard, as if she were trying to be the most efficient Apartment Building Manager in the world.

Sarah stopped in front of me and said How ya doin? Your heating working, alright? I told her it was fine. And I wondered if she had seen you. I wanted to ask you what had cheered you up so much after that meeting, what realization you'd arrived at in your head that seemed to make everything alright. Even a little better.

I saw him walk back to his room and then off again. He had one hell of chip on his shoulder, she said.

Did he? I asked.

Well. All guys his age do. Especially when they're dating women like you.

Women Like Me? I questioned. And Sarah just giggled and walked on, asking the family with the small little girl if their heating was working well.

Women Like Me? What does that mean? Were we really dating? Dating? At a time like this? A *relationship* in the midst of all of *this*? Not some sort of Partnership to end anything? But the conventional? Dating? What's next? Was he going to give me a Promise Ring?

The idea sat in my throat like heartburn. I wasn't ready (at least I didn't think that I was). When I removed Emotion from the equation, it seemed much easier to criticize the situation. A Man And A Woman, Dating At A Time Like This: When There Was Mass-Produced Bloodshed On The Streets. Then again, what if the world only got worse? When I put my feelings back into the equation, I couldn't deny that you made me feel good. I was struck by you. And no matter what anybody did, no matter how many people were killed, I would still feel that way. Was it Lust? Was it Love? Maybe it was both (just like any budding Romance). Kissing you was like running for shelter under a tree in a thunder storm. Maybe it didn't seem so crazy, after all. Life must have some purely positive moments in it too, beyond the profound Social Movements we crave to espouse.

Optimism

...trick mirror...

Lets go c a happy movie 2night!

That was your text message, two days after the Board Meeting. You couldn't even *call* me on the phone? You had to *text* me in order to ask me out? For someone so confident, sometimes you can be a true coward. I'll give you credit for one thing: I certainly didn't think you would want to see me again, so soon. The simplicity of your excitement was like a little child right before he gets his birthday presents (or a dog about to go play a game of Fetch). When I called you to figure out what time and where, you didn't sound like yourself. You sounded as though you had been pacing around your room and your heavy breath panted over the line.

Alright, I said to you (unsure of what the purpose of this frivolous date would be). It was nice to pretend things were Normal, but what was the point if they actually *weren't*? Things were never Normal. There would always be Violence and (at the very least) there would always be Death. Inescapable. Inevitable. Perhaps you wanted us to live our lives to the fullest? Or maybe you just wanted to ignore Sanity and live in a delusional Dream World, where the best dates always took place at the worst of times.

I watched how my steps changed from the usual path I used to walk around my apartment. I always pace around when I'm talking on the phone and when I'm thinking. I watched how the route I usually took (around the couch, edging my way along the coffee table, making sure not to trap myself like a stick in a narrow spring, then around the back window, then a circle around the kitchen, before starting over near the front door, again) was slowly but surely contorted and re-routed, so that I made a new routine. Now, I went straight from the front door to the other end of the couch, avoided the coffee table entirely, and headed straight toward the bedroom (and then I would circle my bed twice, before heading back to the front door). It was like a switch turned on in my brain and somehow changed my personality through my subconscious routines.

When I got off the phone, I smiled. I was glad that this was turning into some greater connection, not just some fling after a Massacre. So we went out that night and saw a Romantic Comedy (something that I thought you would hate, because I was raised to think that all straight men hated Romantic Comedies unless they were trying to get into their girlfriends' pants). I paid for my own ticket. I'm going to pay for myself. I'm that type of woman. I don't think that Love should be For Sale. I don't think that buying someone Dinner And A Movie is payment for Sex or Affection.

As we entered the theater, I went to the bathroom and I stared at my reflection in the mirror. I had put on makeup in the morning (the mascara gently brushed off on the bags under my eyes) and I wondered if it made me look more pissed off with the world than I really was. I wanted to know how I looked to you. Did I look like a Young Twenty-Something or a Frigid, Barren, Ticking Biological Clock? Was I desperate? Were you planning on taking advantage of me? Were you thinking wonderful thoughts about me, right at that moment? When all I wanted to think about was being numb? Numb. Numb. That's what would have been sublime. To not feel. To not be attached. Everything in life would have been so much easier if I could just walk around, untouched by anything. No Pain. No Love. No Happiness. Everything would go so much quicker and moments like this would never be remembered. I washed my hands and I watched the tired girl wearing makeup, in the mirror. She watched me, too. She gave me a death stare. And she was still and stolid in her glance. She was intense. I wanted to know what people thought she was thinking. How would she act if she knew what they were thinking about her? Once, I looked at a Trick Mirror and I saw myself without realizing that it was my own reflection. I saw the girl in the mirror and I said in my head What A Prissy Bitch. She Must Have No Trouble In Life. Some Brat, I Imagine. A Ton Of Friends, And All... To my horror, I realized that I had judged myself so wrongly, from first glance. I think if I were separate from myself, if there were two of me in this world, they would not get along, very well.

When I came out of the bathroom, I met you in one of the back rows of the movie theater. I'm not going to make out with you, here, I said to you.

And you shrugged your shoulders, saying I like looking at things from the back. You can watch all of the people in front of you react.

I didn't know if you were telling the truth or just trying to escape my accusation. The lights dimmed and it was too late to find out from the light shining in your eyes. I wondered how quickly your pupils would dilate.

The light of the screen reflected on your face like a heavenly touch, some halo in the darkness. You sighed so gravely, as each Character went on a roller coaster ride of emotions. You cried when the Characters cried. You laughed when the Characters made a joke. You lived *their lives*. I wondered why you empathized so greatly with all of their dilemmas, hopes, and aspirations. I wondered if those were things that you had yet to uncover in your own life. Were you unfulfilled?

We sat through the movie, the dark cool theater making us sit closer (as if we were struggling for warmth). The couple on the screen started making love. You put your arm around me and kissed my ear, but I drew back. There was a moment of awkward silence. I cared about you. But I was not sure how much. You took your arm from around my back and connected your fingers like a meditating Buddhist Priest. Finally, you arched your back (turning toward me, resting your hands on the arm rests).

What?

What? you said, back (fed up with my passive aggressive withdrawal). I turned pink and I had to let it out like a deep breath you hold in for thirty-three point four seconds.

I'm just finding it difficult to have a *relationship* while the world is being torn apart by Machines that *eat people*!

You looked at me and sighed deep (just like this *hiiihhh hhhhhaaa aaaaah*, as if you were individually sounding out every syllable possible to man). You rolled your eyes at me. And then stared at the dazzling lights on the movie screen. You had had enough. You got out of your seat and I followed you as you walked out along the aisle (people giving you bad looks for distracting them from their distraction). You exited the theater. I walked quickly, behind you. You walked in the cold darkness, your white breath fleeting against the brick buildings along the sidewalk. I don't know why I followed you. You opened the door for me, under the neon marquee (it was like the archaic subtleties we had been avoiding awkwardly pierced through the façade of trying to be Politically Correct). Maybe we could do it in our mind (Live A Perfect Life, try to act how we thought was Logically Correct) but our bodies were weaker than that.

Was it our bodies? Or our hearts?

We walked out of the movie theater like two aliens just landing from Mars, the darkness and depth of reality too much for us to bear. A cold wind blew (it really was nearing winter). We crept around, trying to escape from the breath of reality in the night.

I stopped you for a moment to say Why do you always break up the miserable with the happy like this? It makes everything seem superficial. We have time to see a *movie,* but we can't stop people from *killing themselves*?

Listen to yourself. Suicide Prevention, right? Well, that means we have to prevent *ourselves* from committing suicide, *first.* The worst thing in the world is a depressed Lifter-Upper.

I followed you in silence, all the way home. I was waiting for you to turn around, for you to lunge at me with giant angry eyes full of piss and rum (fiery for the sake of Life still within them). But you were cold and quiet. You didn't look at me tracing your steps, only a few feet behind you.

I shut your door behind me.

I would do anything to make you smile! you called out in anger, criticizing my seriousness. I could feel you wanting to just take off and leave me standing there, alone.

Be *realistic*! We live in a time of War.

Real? Real? you said. You thought about it. And then walked over to me. You suddenly grabbed me close and you kissed my lips. *This* is Real. Your breath smelled like peppermint, your lips like soft rice paper. You held me closer, your tongue swinging with my lips like a kid swimming in a bathtub. And then you bit my lip, like a dog bites a chew toy and you sucked my neck like a hummingbird sucks nectar (and then sucked it harder, leaving a red mark). *This* is real. Your hand reaching below, parting waves, miraculously crossing the Red Sea to Safe Shore. *This.* Do you feel *This?*

I gasped and finally smiled. Yes.

You kissed me harder and went further. *This. This* is real, you said. Reality is a mixture of dichotomous happiness and depression. It fluctuates quicker than your breaths and sighs. Then my heart beats. Reality is not One Or The Other. Reality is *Both.* In the middle of Pain we feel Love. In the middle of Love we feel pain.

It's a contradiction I argued (and you held me closer and closer, plunging deeper and deeper).

This *is* Reality. You asked me Can't you *feel* it?

Yes. Yes. I can feel it.

…again?…

You played me like   a cello, the bow to the instrument, the rosin on the bow creating a tight sharpness, a tactile pressure, a hard slide (like trying to run around on a wooden floor with socks on and not being able to). You stopped. And stopped. And stopped. Resuming the same place. You put me down and picked me up again. Spiccato. The bow jumping from the strings. You couldn't read me straight through (my complex lines, my bitter angles). You needed time to adjust your world to mine. You needed to get used to me after a while. We both weren't sure where it was going. I was the Essay you started writing, but put down suddenly when a sound resonated down the hall. I had trouble looking you in the eye. I was trapped inside my head. I wondered if you were daydreaming about me or if you were caught in the moment, as well. I was too afraid to ask. Would This Work? I pondered. I never wanted to tell you. I wanted your innocent smile, your relaxed calm to fold over me like a warm blanket. I didn't want you to have some sort of Epiphany that would stop you from being what you were, from what you would become (what you are, now).

I didn't know if things would work. I didn't know if this

Relationship, or this World (The New World, in our eyes) would ever work (would ever be Good, again).

Again? It's so funny that I say Again, because there really was no Original. We started in the midst of this. This pain and this pressure. There was no Normal to begin with. There was no Sublime Happiness to be found in your eyes that I could relate back (back to a time when there was no destruction). There was always Death. Death was always mandated by the government. For as long as I or you or our parents could remember. We may like to pretend that Back When We Were Young, Things Were Better Or More Innocent or that we were Living In A Different Type Of World, A Better World, A Calmer World With Fewer Things To Worry About Or Meditate On. But that would be a load of shit. We would be lying. Things were just as bad, before. We were too young to understand the carnage we were raised with (the pain that we were protected from) because we were shielded from the world. But it was out there. We had to open our eyes and see. Learn from it in the Past Tense, learn from it in the History Books in order to understand that our own perspective was not adequate. But then the realization came. And we understood that the world was never truly Peaceful. Innocence was dead, long before we were born. Our childhood was a Delusion Of Perfection. All we have left now are our Dreams.

I want this story to make your eyes sparkle. Your eyes could make these beautiful beams of light, if only you looked into your infinite possibilities. Your eyes would make new lines, expressions, wavelengths. It would be the most amazing fireworks show ever seen. Light would explode in your eyes (like oil in a burner) rising like a mushroom cloud only to sink like a stone or a piece of bread tossed into a large mass of water. I felt so calm with you. All inhibitions escaped me until I tumbled painlessly (expressing all of my inner emotions, my tongue flailing like a typist's fingers on a keyboard). Did you feel it all? Tell me that you felt it with me. Tell Me. I would never have disturbed your lightning. I would never have stilled or startled the symphony of your eyes (your eyelashes would have become tongues in a dramatized brilliance). It would have been so great. But you were so wonderful, already.

...thinking for years...

Wake up time.

Wake Up, I said. We were sitting in bed, staring at the news on TV. I was drinking some coffee and you were flipping pages of the newspaper (making a rustling noise as if you were running in the woods from cannibals, but trying not to make any noise, so no one would find you).

But I'm awake, you said.

I meant another type of Awakening. It was like the first time that I learned about the Machine. It was not the morning. My eyes were already awake. I'd been working for hours. Thinking for years. The day was already partly through. We were already in existence. Our eyes were opened by the Fruit Of The Tree Of The Knowledge Of Good And Evil. But suddenly, the news of the Machine seemed to open my eyes, even wider. Something seemed to poke at me and bring me into True Existence.

But I *am* awake, you repeated.

Me too, I said. And you stared at me quizzically. You weren't sure where I was going with this. *Was she hiding something from me?* you thought to yourself. But I wasn't. A jolt went through my body, like when you jump into the waves in the Pacific Ocean (like volts of electricity pricking my finger tips with spikes of energy). You looked at me. You didn't know what to think. I realized that my body, my mind, my Soul had been re-energized to do this. To Fight The Machine. To go on with our lives. To use our lives for something better than ourselves. I told you all this and you looked at me.

But we're pretty important, too, you said. Remember?

No. I know that, I said. I'm just saying that the world isn't *centered* on us.

But we need to be *in* this world to fix it. We're a big part of this world. (It was as if you were begging with a higher force) People need *Us.*

I don't know if I agree...

I don't mean to sound selfish or narcissistic or something like that. But *listen* to me. I'm not into *any* of that Self-Sacrifice, Suicide Bomber bullshit. We need to live. That's what's important. Alright? So forget about the Cause Going On Without Us. *We* are the Cause.

We Are The Cause?

We're it, babe. You slid your hand down the small of my back, as if we were dancing horizontally. If you don't see your life for what it really is, that your life is just as important as anyone else you're trying to convince, anyone else you are trying to save, by telling them that *their* lives matter, then we're *lost*. The first thing that you need to do is believe it yourself. Can you do that?

I can sure as hell try.

Try then, you said. And you kissed me.

You made me think. You made me think about all those School Dances that I went to wearing a crinoline with unpopular boys wearing satin bow ties. I felt really sorry for them. It wasn't that I was Popular or that they saw me as doing them a favor. They liked me and I went with them because I felt bad that it wasn't mutual. You made me think of that.

And then you reminded me Don't give me any of that Guilt Complex stuff. You hate Pain and Death just as much as the next person. You don't want it for Yourself and you don't want it for Anyone Else. And no one else wants it for you. You want to fight for something? Fight for yourself.

Fight For Myself? You made me think of guys in College who wanted to sleep with me in a dorm room without privacy, with people shuffling in and out. And that heartbreak ate me alive. You made me think of cheap thin sheets on wilting dorm room beds. You made me think of headaches, muttering backaches, and then uncomfortable positions. And when I said No, when I said that I didn't want to do it on the first date, when I didn't want to do it without any privacy, when I said Let's Wait, I wouldn't hear from them again. They got a New Girlfriend. One that would put out, the next night. One they didn't have to wait for. And then they spread crabs all over campus. You made me think of winning out in the end, even though I had to face emptiness to get there. You made me think of how Non-Violence doesn't mean Not Doing Anything.

Fight for myself. With a pen and a paintbrush.

I could sure as hell try, I said to you.

You better sure as hell do *something*.

You rolled over in bed and didn't move. You must have stared at that wall for at least ten minutes. Why were you so fed up with my approach, so far? Were you just pissed off that I wasn't doing more? I grabbed you and swung you around, back on the mattress, and I placed myself on top of you. You stared at me in surprise.

Alright, I said. No more of this passive aggressive *bullshit.*

...seen his horns...

We came up with a new plan. We would guide tours, so that people could actually see what was going on as the Machines killed people. No Anesthesia. No Nothing. Just plain old Murder Machinery.

On a rainy Monday, we filled out yellow Application Forms to become Machine Technicians. We couldn't apply at the local Factory. We had to go to the government building (downtown) to fill out the Applications. Much like the dust-colored walls you first appealed to, the government building (downtown) received us with the same vitality and comfort. The ceiling dripped of beige briefcases and cigars. The fluorescent lighting reflected off cubicles from which hung pictures of a smiling President, oblivious to the Moral Consequences associated with the destruction that occurred in his own country (the destruction of millions of lives, of people that mattered as much as he did). People say there's an Inequality Problem in this country. Damn their perception into our Society, how blatantly obvious that our system is discriminatory (that's all it was ever supposed to be).

The Cubicle Workers looked like your and my parents (graying mother and fathers in their late fifties, early sixties). People that dreamed of retirement only to find that to even afford funeral costs they would have to work for another twenty years, post mortem. As the Concierge of this fine establishment directed us to the first in a long line of manila tables to fill out different forms and take pictures (like the DMV, only worse) an old, plump woman passed us between two desks where we started to fill out Forms For Identification. She carried two stacks of paper, and wore a yuppie Nineteen Eighties suit that she didn't seem to have taken off, in years. You wonder if she's ever taken it off in bed. I wonder if she's ever taken it off to go to the bathroom. The old woman nods at me like she knows the feeling of selling her Soul to promote a system she once thought was just, but wasn't so just any more.

She thinks the man behind the table is the Devil, I whisper to you and you blushed.

She knows, you answered. She thinks she has seen his

horns.

The woman approached us and we went quiet. Don't take the pen, she muttered with her eyes like some Witchdoctor, some ancient Healing Woman trying to warn the younger generation of their naïveté, of their vanity. How ridiculous to think that our generation can out live the perils of hers. A Western Society once based on the belief of children surpassing their parents has died. She knows. She's lived through it all. Her wrinkled skin outlined the Wars that she'd persevered through, filled out the paper work for (permitted to happen). The melanoma on her arms was like a Connect-The-Dots to some buried treasure of her past, long forgotten (some Dream, some Artistic Dream). She wanted to be a Painter. No. A Dancer. But screw that. The Sixties were gone, she had reminded herself. And she wanted a Family, and she wanted Women's Rights, and she wanted to put her foot in the Workplace and make change from the Inside. She knew me, alright. She *was* me. Forty years earlier. She was me in the Past. I knew she was thinking this. It was dictated to me through the insignificant dimple on her right cheek. The scar on her neck. Her smeared lipstick.

You did not see me wink at her. I wanted her to know that this is all a Game. She jutted her head back a little. She wasn't ready for that response. I wanted to tell her about the images that she was missing out on, when she could have lived her life the way she wanted to. How she could have worked for Equality without giving a piece of herself up to the Machine. Her arms were just conveyer belts, feeding the production of the Machine. Looking at her go, I messed up her day. She wouldn't forget my wink (my out of the ordinary sign of Noncompliance).

You saw my eyes straying from the desk and clasped my hand for me to focus. It was hard for me to pretend. You were much better at it. You smiled and tilted your head, unafraid of asking dangerous questions with a smile.

Will we get to see and do everything that goes on with the Machine?

The fat man behind the desk nods. Yes, yes.

What are the Benefits?

I chuckled and you stared at me, menacingly. You wanted me to be serious, not to read into the underlying meaning.

What is the Pay? you kept going. Do we get Health Coverage?

My face turned a little red from holding in a snicker and you gave me another evil glance.

Is there any sort of Compliance Form that we have to sign that guarantees that we end our life via Machine?

I got serious.

Well, said the man behind the counter. It's highly *recommended*, but not required, that you sign a Waiver that permits the government to harvest your body for Energy.

Not *required*, though? I asked. And with a nod (No) I smiled and took a long, deep breath out.

But again, the man said, it's highly *recommended*. Many long standing Employees decided to do so. Why don't I give you the form so you can think about it?

Thank you, you said, taking the blue form (blue for Tranquility, so the people reading it or the people who couldn't read it would get less upset, I assumed). What nonsense. The Psychology Of Persuasion. I remembered Monty Python's *Death Or Cake?* Cake, please. Every time. Every time.

As we walked out of the building you grabbed my waist and told me You did an *okay* job pretending. I knew you were upset.

I'm sorry, I muttered under my breath.

It's alright. We'll get them, next time.

Next Time? What? Wasn't that it? I don't want to go back there, again.

They have to review our Applications. Check our Backgrounds. And then if we Pass, we have to go through another Application. At the *specific* Factory branch. Another close Interview. And training…

Training? My mind wandered. What training?

Well, you said. They're not just going to let us in there and assume we *know* how to kill. We'll have to *learn*. You gave me a glazed-over, shock look. Unpaid Apprenticeship, you clarified.

What? An Internship! Unpaid? We're not even being *paid* to kill people? This is ridiculous. Why would anyone chose to work at this job?

Well. The Benefits *are* great. You get an easy Retirement. You crumbled up the blue *Retirement By Machine* flyer and threw it into the trash (two points). And some people get some sort of Moral Humanitarian Bliss from it. They think that they're *Bettering Our Country* by *Ending The Energy Crisis.*

Energy Crisis, I said under my breath. This is one hell of an Energy Crisis. All the human energy in the world that could have been used for good, for Peace Making, for doctors healing people, for Anything! And what do we reduce it to, instead? We end unemployment by allowing people to kill each other or be killed.

...the best reputation...

Two weeks, an additional Application, and an Interview later, we were in the heart of the most deadly government project in the world. We worked for the Machine so that we could get inside and expose it. We would destroy the Machine. Put a wrench in it to break it. Anything.

You warned me Whatever you do, don't get tricked and sucked into the Machine. Don't become part of the Machine.

Don't worry, I reassured you.

Our first day at Training consisted of long, exhausting, unpaid, menial work. The smell was the first thing that got to me. It smelled like rotten eggs and ammonia, like boiling chemicals were burning, melting flesh.

You know; you covered your nose and whispered into my ear. They train Soldiers, this way. Before War. They make them work the Machines. You see up there? You pointed to the man in the room filled with dials, above our head. This was an Observation Room with a huge window overlooking the Machine. You see him? He's in the Army Reserves. And he's being trained here, before being put into battle. To build up his *stamina*.

Why? I asked you. Why this?

The crew-cut boy standing in the Observation Room (fiddling with knobs) was obeying orders, perfectly. He wasn't even flinching. He must have been nineteen-years-old. He was just a child and he had learned to act with such precious effectiveness. With perfect, apathetic responses to Pain. How to kill just like a Machine. He *was* a Machine. He was just as bad as the contraption in the room, grinding human flesh. He was just as horrible. No. Worse. Because he once was Human, but he'd lost it all. He'd been eaten away by the Machine, just like any other Soul. He was not Human. He was a Military Appliance, no better off than a Tank or a Torpedo. The military did not need rational, moral individuals. The military needed a group of idiots. Soulless, soul-sucking Machines. The military needed *killers*, not *men*. The military needed Deviants Of Natural Law.

THAÏS H. MILLER

Criminals. Not people. Not Human Beings. The military needed
Killing Robots, and those who were cruel enough to produce
murdering Machines.

I smelled thick blood (like butter). And then I *saw* blood.
Running in and out of tubes in a room connected to the Machine,
itself. I heard breaking bones (crunching). And then (yes, then) that's
when I heard it. Screams. They made my skin sizzle. I didn't know
what they were, at first. Most of the other workers wore headphones
or seemed to tune it out. But then the screams became more audible,
until each syllable was as precise as a gunshot.

Ah! Oh God! Help Me! Please Stop! Ah!

I knew what it was and that it wasn't imaginary. I threw up
and started crying in the corner. The next day, we brought a tape
recorder and documented the terrific yelling.

Oh God! Why?!

Stop! This Isn't What I Wanted! Please!

Oh God! God!

AAAAAAAAAAAH! AAAAAAAAAAAAH!

*Stop! You Killers! Stop! Help! Someone Damn It! Can't You
Bastards Hear Me?!*

I'm Burning Alive!

We recorded the noises of the machine too:

CRACK CRACK CRACK

CRASH

TZZZZZZIT TZZZZZZZIT

GGGGGRRRRRGGGGG

SSS IS ISSS ISSS

MRRRRGGGGGGGGG

BEEEEEEEEEEEP

SCREEEEEEEECH

The little boy studying for War did nothing, I did not see his
eyes blink or his hands move to stop it. I saw some sweat drip down
his neck and his palms, if he didn't do it fast enough. As if speed was
the answer for this type of thing (if he couldn't stop it, he could make
it go *faster*, make sure murder was done sooner, instead of having to
live with the moral consequences longer, instead of having to truly
endure the pain). The only painful part for him was waiting for a
Coffee Break. Some loud speaker yelled out certain controls for him
to pull and he pulled them all with the utmost accuracy. I was amazed
that he was not on some sort of Pills or Drugs. How could he not be
sedated through all of this turmoil? What a freak! What kind of

Human Being could do that? That wasn't some kind of *Man*, though, I reminded myself. That was a *Machine*. I imagined this must have been what the Nazis felt.

All of the Upper Management was made up of special doctors (intellectuals trained to be without emotion during all types of Human pain). They listened to the screams all day. Quantifying them. Measuring how many would die and how many volts would come out of their membranes. They were measuring Death with their cannibalistic fingers. Our Coworkers must have felt numb, after awhile. Dead to it all. You and I didn't talk, during work. We just listened. We wanted to reach into those Machines and grab those people as they roasted in oil (if only that meant that our hands wouldn't be simmered off, as well).

As I worked in a dark corner (wiping up trace amounts of excrement, blood, and Human tissue that had spilled onto the floor from one of the large hoses linked to the wall) I started to gag. I made sure that no one saw me. I had to hide behind one of the conveyers. When I was done, I wiped my mouth of the bile and saliva. I went back to mopping. And no one seemed to notice. So I had done my part in covering up and hiding all emotion well. I kept sweeping. It was hard to hear my own thoughts over the roar of the Machine. It was hard to keep my eyes off the carnage, as well. I no longer thought Inner Thoughts, I only remembered the images in my mind of people being torn to bits on the first conveyer belt (their eyes still rolling in their heads) before being put onto the second (in which they were boiled and their organs converted). The Machine was so gruesome. Like some Cut And Run Job. Smash And Boil The Body, Suck It Dry, and then Dispose Of The Waste. It made it seem like graveyards were garbage heaps. I'd never felt so disgusted in all my life. I became disgusted by the small parts of my body, the way my cells arranged into small designs, closely bound together, permitting only a certain amount of sweat to pass through and nutrients to pass in. It was little things that started to get to me, that made me twitch, scratch, and then bite at my skin hard enough to make it bleed.

During our Lunch Break, you held my hand under the white painted, metallic table when you noticed my pale complexion, shaking, and lack of appetite. You squeezed my hand *hard*. As if you were trying to pump Life back into it (like some sort of pulse, some sort of breath or shock). With each hard touch and grasp, you desperately tried to rekindle something into my Soul. I wanted to tell you that I *hated* you. But somehow, your kind grasp (that symbolic care in the mysterious darkness below our tuna sandwiches) kept me from lashing out at you, just then. I still believed this was a Proper Method for us to Stop The Machine.

Our second, third (ninth, twelfth, fifteen, et cetera) days of Training would be the same. The Torture Of The Work Day. No Food At Lunch (but sustenance from a hand held under the Lunch Table). We didn't even look at each other. It would have pained me so much to see the emptiness in your eyes, or for you to see the bags under mine (from the sleepless nights, fearing the dreams, the nightmares, that would come to pass). That squeeze, that vital proof of your existence, your survival under the body that now tolerated so much pain and murder. That was your Soul calling out to me. For an hour, each day. That was how I knew you weren't a Machine, too. That there was still a person inside of that tired, sick, angry body. That there was a purpose behind all of this.

Our Training over, we started Work. You told me According to some of the other Employees, there is only one way to keep our jobs, the first week. We have to prove to the Boss that we're completely apathetic and we would do *anything* for the job. That we would do *nothing* to stop it.

But *all* we want is to stop it. How can we do this? I asked you. How can we Stop Them and Give Them What They Want, at the same time?

You decided to stage something. You decided that you would jam the Machine and that one of us (or both of us) would go in (fix it) and make it start running, again. The catch was that we would release a few people that were entering into it, without anyone knowing, and then put in fake corpses, so that no one would suspect that we had saved a few lives.

First, you decided to place a large wrench into one of the major gears of the Grinding Cycle of the Machine. As a man went in screaming for his life, the Machine already eating the majority of his left leg, the Machine suddenly stopped.

Damn it, Rookie! Yelled out some of the Employees. What have you done this time? Go and fix it!

And so you went gladly and volunteered. You took a sack with you (filled with an already dead corpse) and you told the man in the Machine to lay down very quietly inside of the bag while you replaced him with the dead one. The man whispered *thank you thank you thank you thank you* into your ear. You told him to keep quiet, so that no one would suspect. You took him out and fixed the Machine. But as the Machine started running again, one of the men yelled out, There's A Dead One In There! We Can't Harvest That! Another Employee told me to go into the Machine and fish the dead body out (it was half consumed, one half already sucked into the gripping metallic jaws of the Machine). And I had to climb inside, use my entire body to start to pull it out. Only the torso came out, leaking black decayed entrails behind it (the acid stained the conveyer belt, leaving a hole). Suddenly (as I fixed the jam) the Machine started to work again. With me inside of it. I screamed my ass off.

Get Me The Fuck Out Of Here! I yelled and I yelled, clinging to the dead torso for support (its smashed bones and fingers hugged around my body, its black entrails staining my uniform). The conveyer belt continued to move. And another man (strapped in) went through the same jaws, very quickly, his fresh blood oozing everywhere, his screams under his crushed flesh so much more present in my memory (in my *sight*) than anything behind the metallic cage. I felt the weak pulse in his finger tips as he slid under the conveyer belt. I ran in the opposite direction.

Goddamnit It! Help Me!

I saw the long arm of someone outside grab me and the torso, pulling us upward to get out of the hull of the Machine.

Are you alright? the man with the glasses asked me, amazed that I was still alive.

I'm fine. I'm fine, I told him, still clinging to the torso. Someone tried to grab it from under me. Stop it! He's mine, damn it! I said, as if I were holding a new born child.

How did that one die *in* the Machine, asked one of the Employees, staring in awe at the torso.

Must have had a heart attack or a stroke or something, while it was on the conveyer belt. That shit happens, nodded another one.

Dripping in blood, acid starting to leak though my Uniform, I pushed my body past the Employees, and I ran. I ran and I ran for the nearest Exit. And then I ran toward a dumpster. I ran and I put the body in the dumpster, afraid that someone would do an Autopsy to find the Cause Of Death. Afraid that they would see that it wasn't the young body of the man that had signed the Consent Form to be put in the Machine, but that it was, in fact, a much older body, a ninety-year-old man that had died of Natural Causes, years ago. No. They could never know. They could never know.

I started to strip myself out of my own clothing, the

Uniform which was now being quickly eaten by the voracious acid. As I threw the clothing into the Biohazard dumpster, I watched as the acid not only consumed my Uniform, but started to burn through the old male body, as well. People walked out of the Factory and just stared at my partially naked body, covered in black entrails and excrement. I was now the sole survivor of the Machine. And people just stared and stared.

What The Fuck Are You Fucking Looking At? I yelled back at them. Well, God Fucking Damn It! Haven't You Ever Seen A Woman Drenched In Blood Before? Haven't You Ever Fucking Seen A Worker Survive A Fucking Repair Job In The Machine Before?

...no... said one man (in shock) trying to answer my question.

I had done it. I had made the Best Reputation that I could.

Get Back To Work! I told them. And I started to walk inside. You took off your shirt and I wore it to cover my body. It slid open, though, and I tried to pat away the blood, smeared along the inside. The Management watched me from the Observation Room. The Soldier watched me from the Observation Room. Their mouths were gaping open, the jaws ajar. They had no idea what to make of this.

What was it like? some woman asked me. And I told her *Go Fuck Yourself.* I think she obeyed, because she quickly scampered off to the ladies room.

I think that did it, you said to me in a hushed tone, so that no one could hear. Finally, we had made the reputation that was needed. Finally, we could be trusted, so that we could start to work *against* the Machine. Who would ever believe that the girl that so vigorously fought for the Machine's *repair* would ever want to *destroy it,* in the end? Finally, when we built up a reputation with Management for being Loyal, Desensitized Employees, we could start to break the system from the inside.

...the villain in a bad dream...

We gave our first tour to Gerald Hanasee, a rich businessman investing his company's money in Machine Assembly, to check if the product fit into his Corporation's Code Of Social Responsibility. Also attending were Mr. and Mrs. Johansson, and their two children,

Bobby and Julie. Mr. Johansson was a big fan of the new source of Energy because it was keeping his small, Computer-Software Company afloat. He encouraged his wife and children to Retire By Machine, as he planned to do, after he turned sixty-five. Because It's Just Downhill From There, he noted. In addition, three medical students (Yolanda Parker, Tasha Maxwell, and Bernadette Harper) decided they wanted a first hand look at the major improvements the Machine was causing. They planned on using this tour for a term paper assignment, but they were also considering interning at a Machine Plant.

We're looking into running Machines for a profession. Tasha brushed off her shoulder with that remark.

The group's corkscrew smiles disappeared like sand in an hour glass as we took each step a little further into the building. After they heard the screams (as well as the turning and cranking of the Machine cracking Human bones) Mrs. Johansson grabbed Bobby and Julie and ran. Mr. Johansson just looked at you and me, in pale shock. I think we smiled, now that he knew. How could we smile when we were corrupting these Innocent People? What did they ever do, in their simplistic lives, to deserve two tour guides like us? Maybe being Ignorant was enough of a crime.

I watched as Mr. Johansson recognized the sound (like you first did when you heard the Machine). It sounds like a beetle being smashed against a hot sidewalk. No. No. A snail, shriveling when smothered in salt (or perhaps an ant being burned by a magnifying glass, in the sun). Humans recognize the sounds of murder like the sound of a baby crying, through the pulling of some biological trigger we never knew we had.

So, this is the Death Penalty, now, Mr. Johansson said, as if trying to search back to the roots behind this madness.

Actually, sir, you spoke up, the Machine is not only used for Convicted Criminals or Volunteers. It is also used to Euthanize those deemed Wards Of The State.

You mean the Mentally Ill? Yolanda asked.

Mentally, the Machine must be much more painful that Shock Therapy. It must be like a violent thrashing. A Lobotomy where you are awake, alert, alive, and feeling every minute of the pain associated with the juices in your head being squeezed out of you like a lemon. How would that feel? I asked.

I can't imagine, Bernadette answered. I don't want to.

People like to think about things that they can't do, that are

Against The Rules. But what if all of the inhibitions were lost? And what if people had no boundaries? Would people really go through with it? What if Brad Pitt was available to every housewife in every bedroom? Would she really sleep with him? What would her husband think? What about her children? How would she explain that she had an affair, just because she had the opportunity? It is the same way with Death. Would you do it? Would you commit Suicide, if it were easy? If it were just a breath away? A finger tip, a pen, a signature away? Would you sign your Life away, if you really could? Would you do it, if everyone else was doing it? What if it was a fad? If people told you, *in person* and in *the media* that it was Sexy? I'm not sure what you would think, if you were raised in a world like that, where the Forbidden was easily accessible. What would you do? What would you do, if you didn't know any better?

There were no pauses, no moments for Silence or Reflection Over The Loss Of Life. No. This was a Factory, complete with wires, hulls, compartments, levers, radiators, and (most importantly) Machines. About twenty Machines lined up, one next to the other, waiting to consume Raw Material. These Machines hungered and panged. When small pieces of bones or Human entrails were trapped in their hulls, the Machines whined and groaned like any full-fledged adult with heartburn or an upset stomach. These Machines were cannibals, consuming the original Machine-Like Organism, itself. The Machines had their own language. They whistled shrilling high-pitched notes that ruptured a Human eardrum. The walls oozed with Human leftovers that manifested into workers' terror and guilt. Guilt over the loss of Human flesh and the lack of remorse other Humans had for it.

Our tour group passed a herd of Cleaners. The Cleaners of the Machines walked around in white plastic suits, spattered with blood and Human entrails. They wore heavy masks that protected them from any infection. Outside the room with the Loading Dock for Human bodies, the Factory was spotless. If those other rooms and offices were anything, they were *clean*. The Cleaners did a sublime job, making sure that every corner of the other rooms was *sanitary*. Other than the sounds, this Factory was as bland as any other building in the country.

Then, I opened the door to the Loading Dock.

This is where the *real* action happens, I said in a sinister voice (with sexual overtones that everyone seemed to understand). This was the Most Important Room Of Them All. The Conveyer

Belt Room. Where people were strapped, after signing Benign Waivers in a cutesy clean Lobby. The tour group gave me funny looks. And then they looked in front of them. A young woman was strapped to a metallic slab, struggling desperately to get free as the Machine started to chomp down on her knees. The conveyer belt was in front of dozens of sharp, vicious blades and crushing hammers. My group watched as the people in front of them were smashed to death, their excess blood squirting in all directions and eventually draining to the floor. The carcasses were quickly sucked into a boiling acid vat. The Cute Outsiders had just walked in on a Real Life Horror Film.

I wondered about our tourists (their shaking knees and uneasy stomachs). Yolanda threw up in a trashcan (coincidentally filled with fat enzymes). A piece of Human tissue spattered on Mr. Johansson. And as he sighed, a piece of newly expelled skin touched his lips. He sucked in his breath, trying to get a handle on the situation. Then, Bernadette and Tasha stepped away, unblocking him from a large amount of spray. Mr. Johansson was drenched in another man's blood.

An older man was put onto the conveyer belt next. He screamed before dying Wait! This Isn't What I Wanted! I Changed My Mind! Only to be told by the men strapping him in that It's Too Late, You Already Signed The Form. This is why we brought the tour group here. To see the Consequences to their Actions. Behind our group's plastered shut eyes, their minds had been exposed to the truly grotesque and would have to endure these images forever, passing them on to their children. Our group was like a test tube of small seedlings, infused with transgenic material that would change them and their offspring for generations. They were Damaged Goods. We had *fucked* with them. Our group would have psychological problems from which they might never be able to recover. Our group would have Post-Traumatic Stress and Depression. They would have episodes of Severe Aggression and Sadness, at the same time. And all I could do was look at you and wonder if we were really doing the right thing. We'd expose the Machine's inner workings, but did we expose our own, as well? How could *we* endure doing *this* to other people? Were people really so heartless in the end? Did people even care about Visceral Kindness or Actions Of Righteousness And Justice, anymore? *Was* this Justice? It didn't feel like it. Tasha fainted. And we quickly cut the tour short. All in all, we got the reaction we were looking for. It encouraged us to continue conducting tours.

Our groups usually consisted of fat men wearing shorts, with cameras around their necks, dragging their apathetic children. We decided to have a New Policy. We would play the recording of screams before we entered the Factory, and would no longer permit children under the age of seventeen to enter. Parents didn't understand.

It's like an NC-17 rated movie. Except in real life, you said jokingly. But I didn't smile. This only encouraged those looking for an orgasmic experience to attend. I don't want to remember the guys I saw masturbating behind the building, *before* we went in.

Our Boss, Dr. Hum, liked the idea of offering tours. He wanted to discuss our Operations. In his dusty office sat a desk cluttered with pictures of his wife and three children. There was one of the whole family on a hunting trip, Dr. Hum holding up his big kill (a baby deer). I couldn't believe that a man like that, just that Thursday afternoon, had overseen the killing of hundreds of people. And that meant nothing to him. Nothing to worry about. He had a wife and three kids. I imagined that if I were his mistress, I would play terrible tricks on him. For example, in the midst of fornication I would stick his penis in my ass and defecate on him, dispelling waste all along his most precious parts, making him seize with uncontrollable convulsions of nausea and disgust. His lower jaw would be torn down in an awful surge of unhappiness. I would giggle. I had other dreams, too. I would dream that while in the middle of sex, I would call out his mother's name, I would rub poison ivy all over his penis, I would bite him and draw blood, I would tie him to his bed and make the dog run all over him. Or I dreamt that I would smother him in the vomit-covered blankets of his small children. I would dump his head in the toilet. I would stick things up his ass, while he was sleeping. I would put laundry detergent or cleaning fluid in his pipe. Soak his cigarettes in kerosene and ammonia. Or make fake cigarettes filled with hair! Hair from the drains of his god-forsaken home! From his shower drain! From his hand sink! I would collect his pubic hair and make him smoke it! I would shave his eye brows, while he slept. I would spit on him and put tattoos on his arms and legs while he slept a toxic, pill-induced sleep. Screw the *Formalities*. We'd be open about our fake, unnatural, drug-induced existence. Up When We Want To Be, Down When We Want To Be. Isn't it insane that we could control our every feeling, without an External Substance? I would take away the Pills. And I would make him try to live the Natural Existence that he would so often crave and vote for, in all those elections. He would cry, those sleepless nights. He would drone, those sleepy mornings. I would bite his tongue, if he tried to kiss me. I would put toe nail clippings, and dandruff-treating shampoo (or worse! Stain Stick!) in his cereal. I would watch him vomit in the toilet, lying on the bathroom floors I had lathered with fish guts and lighter fluid. I would do *anything* to make that man scream!

Now, let me tell you. You two are really Entrepreneurs! Dr. Hum exclaimed. What an idea! Spreading the Word to all those people out there who don't know about the wonders that this Machine is doing! You too are the Missionaries, the Converts Come To Spread The Light! I'll be the Priest! Dr. Hum thought about it some more. He looked at the Propagandist Poster on the wall, advertising the *Wonders Of The Machine*. It's not enough, he mumbled to himself, looking at the anorexic white ballerina in the picture (the dancing girl's muscular body outlined in a sheer white tutu, an Emblem of the Immaculate, Pure, White, Innocent Work Of The Machine). That Emblem Of The Machine reminded him of the perfect body he once had. He keeps his old Football Trophy, nearby. On the Trophy is a chrome football quarterback. Dr. Hum remembered the days before the surgery. Before that final play at State. Before he tore all those ligaments and was told he would never play football again. He remembered sitting in the white hospital bed, eyeing all of the test tubes near the cancerous man in the bed, next to him. He wanted to play with those tubes like his own organs (like he would get some sexual rise from somehow screwing with this man's only means of survival). That's when he changed his Major to Chemistry. He remembered such good days from his alma mater (mostly spent killing rats in a Science Lab). Dr. Hum was fat and middle-aged now, with a futon instead of an office chair, in his study. He stared around the dusty office, the light desperately trying to stream in through the Venetian blinds. Dr. Hum stood up and quickly shut the blinds. Too much light, he muttered, pondering over those lost, dark days. Dr. Hum's stubby hands fingered the Trophy of his glory days. He felt the perfect chrome, masculine body. He wanted that Perfection. He wanted his *Time* back. He wanted Everything and he'd do Anything for it. The Prestige. The Glory Of Those Old Days.   Finally, Dr. Hum came to a conclusion about our endeavors. I think you two should charge *money* for tours.

We got home late that night, blood stains on our shoes. Charge Money! Charge Money! Damn it! What an idea, you said sarcastically, pretending you were him. But it was too much for you. This is such bullshit!

How are we doing anything *right?* We're just helping to benefit him *and* the government! I paused for a moment. And I looked at your face. Lines could be traced, circling around your forehead to your chin. It was as if we had lost years of our life in this madness, this stupid Career Choice For Change. I looked at the dark bags under your eyes (dry like a desert and bereft of all tears). We were Immune. We Didn't Feel Anything. We strapped people onto conveyer belts and watched them die. We stood in a glass room and made sure that all those little levers worked, that all those timers were clicking. We traced where and how much of the New Energy was being dispersed throughout the city. That Energy was powering *our* apartment building and we weren't doing *anything* to stop it. I looked at you and I didn't even like you. I looked at you and I just saw another body that I would eventually feed on a conveyer belt into a Machine. It wasn't Love. It wasn't for Survival. I was no longer Human. I was standing there, looking at another Human, mapping out exactly what I could get out of harvesting your body (out of destroying you). I looked straight into your weary eyes and I told you I can't do this, anymore.

What? you asked me. My hair clumped to the back of my neck.

Listen to me:

I can't *do this,* anymore. I can't do this Solution. This Solution Is *Shit!* It doesn't work! It just makes me part of a Machine that rips people's bodies apart! And I'm giving fucking Tours! And I was giving them to fucking Children! What the fuck is wrong with you? My hands rose to my face as I approached you, my knuckles white as I clenched them tight. You motherfucking sadist! Fuck you! You brought me closer to the problem! You motherfucking *bastard!* You make me Help Them! I fucking hate you! Fuck! I punched you in the face. I wanted to rip your skin apart, like all those people dying in that Machine running, all day, every day.

You grabbed my hands strongly and I fought to get them out of your tight fists.

You're tired, you said. You don't know what you're saying, now.

If anything, *you* were tired. Of anyone giving up. You had devoted your Soul to fooling the government into giving in. Giving in to their malicious practices. Into kissing their feet. Into feeding their mouths with the amount of glorious blood the Aztec gods once craved. You had resorted to Human Sacrifice. Cannibalism. And most of all, the Loss Of Your Ability To Feel. I could have pricked you with a pin at that moment and you wouldn't have felt a thing. You were *numb*. But to tell you that I was Giving Up. You felt *That*. You felt my surrender, more than just as a punch to the face. You felt it like someone had scarred you in the face with a glistening scalpel, slicing open your forehead in one single blow.

The only thing I'm tired of is *you*! I didn't want to touch that thing! And you have me drenched in blood! Damn It!

I hated you, at that moment. The thought of you made me gag. What you had put me through. What your face constantly reminded me of. You were like the Villain In A Dad Dream. You were bloodstained, sweaty, and rank. You were terrible, just to look at. I couldn't even imagine what your insides looked like (but having seen the intestines of people all day and all week and almost all month long, I knew exactly how they were shaped and how much blood and how much waste, and how much *Energy* could be harvested out of them). The Machine didn't discriminate, although I imagined that your orifices must have been clogged with piles of black and blue bile because of all of the dirty deeds that you had put me through.

We have to bring exposure to the problem, you tried to explain. We have to expose the Machine for what it is!

Whom have we exposed it to? I questioned you. To some *Children*! To some goddamn *Tourists*! Some Medical Students who will return to classes on Monday? What the fuck is wrong with you! You took all the Innocent People in this world and grated their *Souls* in the Machine! I started crying. You son-of-a-bitch. You're just as bad as them... you're just as...

I started weeping. My voice tumbled out of me, until it was as thin as a brush of air. You held me close (like I was a small, huddling chinchilla, seeking shelter from a fur trader) telling me *shhh* and rocking me back and forth.

The government killed him, I muttered... *they* killed him...

Imagines of John rushed back into my head, like a silent movie. We were bicycling in a green neighborhood. I held on to him as we weaved in and out of the shade of the trees overhead. The back of his neck was soft and I squeezed him tighter. Suddenly, I saw my nakedness before his Death. Then the plastic bag the remnants of his body were wrapped in, before he was buried in the coffin. I saw him painting. He looked back at me and smiled and mouthed for me to come closer to him to take a look (that one hurt). I saw our friends creating the Anti-Machine Posters. I saw how our entire Peaceful Movement was obliterated. And how this Peaceful, Pacifistic Movement was falling down the same drain. John. I saw John. John…

Shh…you breathed the sound out, again and again. Shh…

But what if they kill us, too? I looked up to you with red eyes, …what if they kill you? I let my tight first curl around your collar. You were still you in there, deep down, past the blood. You still cared. You were only waiting. Biding your time. Appeasing them until you sought your revenge. But when? When?

They're not going to kill me, you said.

I pushed you away. And I started walking away from you, hitting the sofa on the way toward the back of the room. You don't know that! You don't know anything! You're an imbecile! Why do I even listen to you? I started choking on the tears in my throat. I gagged a little and I grabbed my stomach, as I fell to my knees (prayer position). I wanted to die. You ran toward me, as I headed for the floor. Why don't you just shoot me, now? I looked up at you and you held me so tightly.

I am not going to let anything happen to either of us.

But it already *has*. So much *already* has.

The Kitchen Sink Faucet Was Leaking. You Left The Seat Up In The Bathroom. I don't know why these images suddenly hit me, but it was like we were living in some alternate reality. Every time we cleaned the Machine, my apartment got messier and messier. Every time we smiled at the Boss, we frowned at home. We lived in two worlds. Divided

It's not my fault, you said.

It's *everyone's* fault, I clarified. How are we going to stop *them*?

You dangled there a moment, not knowing what to do (maybe you couldn't solve everything).

I'm just saying, I started to get myself together, that this is about people Modernizing. People Advancing. People Working For Some Greater Good. We can't combat them *their* way. We have to fight them *our* way. We can't use their Human Methods Of Change. We have to use the Supernatural. We have to combat their Physical Change with Mental Change. Emotional. Hell, with Spiritual Change. How can we do that? How can we?

...play along...

So we charged money. A little at first. (I hate when fights result in absolutely no real change). We gave out two types of tours. One in which Adults were allowed to see Everything and one that was rated PG-13. We advertised that our tours were twenty dollars for adults and ten for children, (twelve-years-old and under). Dr. Hum walked by our advertisement (complete with prices) and nodded at you, smiling. A young man (he looked only nineteen-years-old, with blonde hair almost totally white) who had been working at the Factory for only a little while approached us, close to sunset. Hello, honey, he said to me as he came over (you, only a few feet away, raised one eyebrow). My name's Billy, said the boy, brushing the back of his hand up and down my sleeve. I hear you're selling things. I was wondering what's for sale.

Can't you read? I said. We're selling Tours.

Tours To The Sexiest Machine, In Action, his voice was exaggerated and excited. He seemed young and innocent, but terribly confused. I wondered if he was medicated (he seemed to have come straight from a Psychiatrist's couch). I bet those tours get mighty lonely, he said coming closer to me.

Hey, you said, grabbing his arm. Don't touch.

Okay, Daddy-o, he said to you, laughing. I just want a little love from Mommy. Is that so bad? He started to fake cry. What's so bad about loving Mommy? Oh God! I love her! I love her! Daddy is going to hurt me! I just want some love! I just want someone to love me! Touch me! He pretended to faint on the sidewalk. He put his head on your shoulder. But then again, Father And Mother Is Man And Wife; Man And Wife Is One Flesh And So My Mother. *Come*, For England! He jutted his groin toward you.

Looks like we got Billy The Bard, on our hands, you said to me.

Billy got up and took a bow, some people in line applauded a little. Thank you. Thank you he said and approached me, kissing my hand. You are *both* lovely Players.

Who are you? I asked, cringing at his saliva.

What are you? is more like it, you interjected.

What Am I? Why, I am a man, sir. And so are you, he said and then came close to my ear and said.You don't remember me, sweetheart? Has it been that long since we both saw John?

I drew my breath for a minute, trying to remember who he was. Billy. Billy. John's sister Joan was an Actor, she had a son out of wedlock that John's parents had shunned. His name was William! William became Billy, I guessed.

Are you Joan's son? Are you John's nephew?

That would be it, darling! Hit it right on the nose! He bopped himself on the nose and fell on the ground, again.

Enough with the theatrics, you told him, eyeing the crowd. Although the line of Tourists enjoyed it, our Co-workers did not.

Honey, he leaned close to me, we're like Family! Come here and give me a little kiss.

You looked very perturbed.

No, Billy. Get yourself together, I told him, pushing him away. What's wrong with you?

Nothing. Baby, I'm just acting, is all. You can't turn me Off and On. Well, maybe only *you* can turn me on On *On*!

What's with this guy? you asked me. I shrugged.

Listen to me, John's Widow, Billy started to speak.

I interrupted him, whispering I'm not John's Widow. He and I never got married, Billy.

Well. You were living together, weren't you? he asked me. Yes…

So. Close Enough. It's called Common Law Marriage. Billy continued, Listen, Wise One. My mommy dearest said that I could find you around here. And I figured knowing how you and John were, you'd still be fighting this thing. I believe in fighting this thing, just as much as you or your Boy Toy over there, he said glancing at you.

Hey! You were insulted by the nickname. I don't even know you.

Now let me help you. I can do great things. I work hard. And I'm easy to get past Guards and the Police and all that. You should see my stash at home! I'm a good kid. Not some punk. I had a Psychiatrist when I was ten, he said I had an Old Soul and that I'm Over eager. Billy started jumping up and down, like a small puppy. He enjoyed the attention and he liked talking to me, like he was right back in his Psychiatrist's Office. Billy wanted me to take notes of his thoughts with my eyes. He just wanted someone to indulge him. And then my Mom, she doesn't care when I smoke a Mary Jane in the house. And never once have I been caught by some Pig Cop, Baby Killer! Never once!

Oh, shit! you said, looking around.

Billy! Billy! Wait! I stopped him from going on. I miss John and I miss your mother. A lot. But you're very young. And I don't want you to get hurt. Why don't you go home and get an Education?

Oh *right*. Billy tried to hide his discouragement with a plastered smile. Education. Like how they Educated Me in High School about how *Noble It Is To Contribute Your Body To Energy*. And about how people like my uncle were Evil *Men*, trying to get in the way of a *Good Cause*. He shifted in his step, passing quickly along the sidewalk, taking his hands in and out of his jean pockets. Yeah, yeah. That'll do it. That'll make me *into* one of them! He did a fake Hitler salute and started to walk away.

I'm sorry, Billy. I'm sorry. I walked up to him and gave him a hug, holding him close. Billy, everything's going to be okay, but we're in the middle of doing something really *tricky* here and I need you to play along. Alright?

Play Along? Billy's eyes glistened. Damn right, it's going to be okay, He separated himself from my arms, facing the two of us. I've come to you because I'm old enough now to fight this awful system and I need some cash in my pocket so that I can start my acting career. Anyway. I could kill two birds with one stone.

...lose a lot of prestige...

Every cent we raised from the Machine Tours went to Anti-Machinocide Publicity (in the form of Commercials that Billy starred in). In one Commercial, he was an Orphan because of the Machine. In another, he was an Energy-Addicted Teenager, playing video games when he suddenly realized that his resources were coming from Human Deaths. He was a brilliant actor. He goofed off a lot (and he read a little too much Freud) but he was a wonderful spinner of words. He reminded me so much of what I had heard about his mother. He must have gotten his acting abilities from her. I never met his father. I always imagine him to be fair in skin and hair color, short, and thin. I imagine that his hands had calluses on them and that he could never shave properly, so he always had a little stubble. I imagine that his legs were short, and that he could never support a voluptuous woman like Joan with his infinitesimally small arms. Most likely, he could never capture Joan's entire being with his body, alone.

Joan told me that he did not leave her but that she took the baby and left him without telling him where they were going. Billy's father wasn't The Type Of Man Who'd Come Looking, Joan told me once over the phone during Thanksgiving (as I stared at John from across the kitchen table). John had no idea of what we were talking about. That would be the moment that John would ask for the phone, so that we would stop talking. But John couldn't ask, anymore. So nothing was interrupted. Not even those horrible stories that qualify as Crossing The Line or Too Much Information. Secrets poured out like rain into a street gutter, muddy and foul smelling.

Billy was still very immature and inexperienced when it came to the realities of what we were doing. He would stop by the Factory, too often (especially as the Commercials became more widespread). He'd usually have some dyed-blonde girl on his arm (some wannabe starlet who had yet to see her name in bright lights, if she was even over eighteen). He wore sunglasses like some young James Dean. One afternoon, after there was a News Report about the Freelance Commercials, Billy decided to appear at the Factory to celebrate. He was immediately bombarded with a hundred fans wanting his autograph. People in line to be killed started to get out of line. This was an amazing technique to stop the Machine's production, because it really worked. At least for the Volunteers. If only just then our Boss didn't see us with Billy. Oh God, if only he had been sick from work that day. When our Boss found out that we'd been using all of the money from the tours on Commercials, he wanted to put us in the Machine, as well.

Billy was arrested on sight for Trespassing, Conspiracy, And Interference With Government Operations. A number of police dogs tore at his leg and when he fell they scarred his beautifully angelic face. He rolled away in the back of a Policeman's car. Billy was transferred to a cell near his home town, I know that much. I wonder if his mother was allowed to bail him out, if her tear-stained stage makeup rubbed onto his pale skin as she greeted him, fervently. I wonder if she was given the freedom to scold him or if he was scolded by the Police Department itself, without her consent. I wonder if Billy is alive. I wonder desperately if he was killed by the Machine. I never heard from him, again.

You and I were dragged into Dr. Hum's office with George, the Machine's Secondary Technician. You see, Dr. Hum lectured us, this is a Business. And when you take money away from the Business and use it for Purposes Discrediting The Business, we lose a lot of

Prestige. And when the Business loses Prestige, then I lose my *Reputation*. And that makes me look Bad. And then I lose more money. And that makes me angry. Do you understand what I mean when I say that you Cost Me A Lot More Than What You Are About To Lose?

What are you talking about? you asked, confused.

George, do you mind taking care of this for me? Dr. Hum said. And the next thing I knew, that fat Machine Worker grabbed you and started to hurl you towards the Machine. Thank God we fought him. Thank God I ripped open his hands and beat his head with a metal shard I found lying on the ground. Thank God we didn't get sucked into the very thing we were trying to fight.

We ran so fast the light couldn't catch us. We hit the Emergency Alarm and the beeping just added to the fierce suspense of the moment. Our realized paranoia chasing us, we jumped down flights of stairs, down the Emergency Exit Routes. We broke the glass from the Fire Hose Box and picked out the axe with our cut fingers, preparing to fight off the giant man with no Soul. Our blood dripped onto the linoleum tiles of the entryway. We then jetted out. Past the long lines outside. Screaming. Running. The people backed away, thinking that perhaps we could be survivors, people from the Dead coming back to reclaim Life. They saw us as Ghosts. And some covered their mouths at the sight of our gushing hands. Little did they figure, there'd be more of that where they were going.

The cold air shocked our bare faces as we stared out into the darkness, shielded by a lone street lamp. We ran into the darkness, finding by memory what we thought was the direction home. We were wrong the first time. We went West instead of North and ended up near some back alleys, as George recruited some of his fellow Workers to hunt us down. We ducked behind a dumpster in an alley with a homeless man and covered his mouth so that he couldn't call out (turning us in for some dreamed-up Reward). I tried to hold my breath so tightly. But I couldn't. I panted and spit into the street. My saliva froze against the side of my mouth. My lungs fluctuated in and out, trying to catch up with my frenzied heart.

We have to get out of here, I whispered to you. And you saw that we had headed in the wrong direction.

Wait for them to pass, you said. And we waited a moment. And then we saw a Police Car slowly pull up by the alley way.

What are we going to do? I panicked.

Shh… You motioned for me to edge toward the dumpster. Get inside.

...the story of mankind...

It was you, me, and the homeless man, crouched in the dumpster; the Police Car in the night outside. For a moment, we sat in complete silence, uncomfortably smelling the decaying, rotting trash around us.

Come here, often? the homeless man asked me (a weird place to hit on someone).

Do *you*? I asked him.

In whispered tones, the man rambled Well. Yes. I grew up only a few miles from here. I was born to a crack addict in a shack the size of a shoe box. My room wasn't much bigger than this here dumpster. My mother got arrested when I was nine. And I got moved from Foster Home to Foster Home, by the courts.

In the darkness, it was hard to make out the lines in his eyes. He seemed so old. He must only have been in his early Thirties but he seemed like he had lived for a hundred years. He was thin and his arm twitched (some Drug Addiction or Mental Illness, I was sure). I sat and I listened to his sad tone of voice drift off to some other plateau of being, as if through the telling of his story, he could escape to some distant place, making his story objective, separating himself from it, entirely. This was not about him. It was not some sob story to be turned into a *Lifetime* Television Movie. It was the Story Of Mankind.

Shh!! I think they're coming, you said.

Let him finish! I said back. And I stared at the homeless man, twitching in the dumpster, his skin wrestling next to ours. Why did you never go to the Machine? What kept you from Suicide all these years?

I don't know. There are better things in life than Sex, right? Like *Living*?" I smiled. This man was a *genius*.

We waited a long time. And finally, the sirens seemed to melt like butter into grits. We stayed in the stench another few minutes, just to make sure.

They're gone now, you said. We should go.

Thank you for living, I told the homeless man. And he nodded his head, attempting to smile. And then kissed my hand. I pulled it away quickly, uncomfortable. I imagined this was his only contact with the Opposite Sex that wasn't For Sale. Probably the only Human contact he'd had, in a while. A chill went over me. Free Love wasn't so free. You saw that I was uneasy and you put your hand on my shoulder, adjusting my body, tilting it toward the end of the alley, pointing in the direction that we had to exit.

Thank you, lady, said the man (as if thanking me for the brief encounter, for listening, for letting him put his spit on me). I felt Guilty. I did not feel like I had done any good deeds, that day. If anything, I had done so many wrong things. Put Billy In Jail. Risked Your Life. Destroyed Our Plan. The homeless man asked me if I came there often. In my mind, I had. (My mind had been in that dumpster for a very long time, in fact). But my body was too numb to show it. That man had to initiate a Conversation, he had to have the Pick Up Line. I stood there speechless for a moment. And then you moved me.

...home with me, under the moon...

Our feet shuffled through the snow on the ground, our minds pulsating, spouting in the air, our breaths outlining our thought patterns (quick balls of smoke that disappeared as soon as we passed). Freedom. Freedom. I could breathe. We paddled our feet past the cold soot around us. I realized that everyone wanted something that they couldn't have. That was what was so enticing. So intriguing. So capitulating. The homeless man in the dumpster wanted to Live, but he wanted Sex, too (it just seemed like he couldn't have both in his life). I imagined Nuns, Priests, Prudes, Asexuals. I imagined how, at night, they must clamor in their beds sometimes, in so much Pain and Loneliness. I thought of the STD Positive Person, sitting in a hospital bed. I thought of him dying from AIDS. Or from Gonorrhea. Or from Syphilis. I thought of how lonely Schubert must have been. His ugly, deformed face. His beautifully sad music. How he slept with a Prostitute because he was desperate for something he couldn't have. Because he was desperate for Love. I reflected on how he had died so young, of Syphilis. And suddenly, I just thought of myself. Lying in bed after John died. Alone. Realizing that all I ever wanted was someone to lie next to me and now I had to be by myself. There was a time when it wasn't about John and it wasn't about Love. A time it was about my Survival (alone in a bed made for two).

You Can't Always Get What You Want, But If You Try Sometimes, You Just Might Find, You Get What You Need. You quoted the Rolling Stones and I smiled, as if you are trying to give me Hope For Our Cause. I needed Hope. I needed some Idealism. I once got into a long argument with a Cackler at a Protest who told me that *Realism Is Better.* That Idealism wouldn't do me any good in this world. That as an Artist, I wasn't doing anything. That I wouldn't *change* Anything. Didn't he know that almost all Social Change is influenced by Artists? Artists (more than any Politicians) tug at the heartstrings of the Public's innermost thoughts. Memories of Bob Dylan's *She Belongs To Me* stuck in my head, from time to time. *She's Got Everything She Needs, She's An Artist, She Don't Look Back.* The words lull my insides and soothe my fiery brain. I imagine if we were ever caught by the Machine, I would sing that song to myself. And perhaps things would be okay, in the end. Maybe I would just tell myself this, to make things not seem so bad. Some Delusion. Some False Ideals in order to survive the pain of losing. Oh, if only they offered *Anesthesia!*

What are you thinking about? you asked me. You look so intense. Your eyes are so wide.

I'm thinking about things that I can't have.

Can't you just be happy? Or fulfilled, at least. Happy with the things that you do have?

What do I have? I asked you.

You have me. That's all you need, you said.

No. That's not All I Need.

You tried to clarify, That's all that's *Important.*

So. *You're* the Most Important Thing In The World, are you? You fell right into my trap.

We are the Most Important *Things* In the World, you said to me. That's what we have to think for *Survival.* You And Me. You And Me are going to change this place or get the hell out of it. Remember my Space Shuttle Idea?

Do we even have enough money?

So we'll be Pirates. Hijack The Shuttle.

What if we don't Survive? I start to be serious. What if we never learn how to regulate the Oxygen Levels, on the Shuttle? Or worse. What if we get eaten by the Machine? Caught by the government before we ever leave?

What if! *What if!* you mocked me. Why do you always play

this *Game*? What if that man's tie were a *Snake*? And that woman's belt a *Lasso*? What if we Lived? What if you Loved Me? What if this Relationship survived, even through the End Of Time? Through Hell? Through the Darkest Side Of Humanity? What if? What If? At least be *Positive*!

I'm *trying* to be Positive. I was just thinking of *all* of the Possibilities. Not just a few. Not just some missed, preconceived Hubris, some step that we overlooked.

Just run home with me, under the moon. (You always were such a romantic). Come with me. Come with me. Come with me…

But what if we don't make it home?

We won't make it home if you keep up all this fucking jabbering. Who knows when the Police will come? Who knows who will hear us and call the Cops? You rolled your eyes at me. You held my shoulder, trying to calm me. Who knows if we will ever remember this? Who knows if we won't go insane tonight, from the stress? You shook your hands violently, trying to make me laugh. Can you remember my *Name*? How many fingers am I holding up?

Would you want to remember? I thought for a moment about all the pain that we had witnessed. Too much for a Lifetime (too much *Forever*). More than having to watch a child in the hospital, or tear dried scabs from your skin. More than injecting yourself with a needle, or sticking yourself with a pin (or having to sew your bloodied pieces back together, again). It was all too much. It was too much Self-Induced Torture. Too much Masochism. It was too *much*.

Please, darling. Please, you whispered in my ear. Stop thinking about it. We're going to get through this. Everything is going to be fine. Shh… shh…

…just run and run and run…

Finally, in the darkness of winter, we returned to your apartment.

I'm so cold, I told you. You grabbed me and held on so tightly (and you rubbed your hands over my shoulders and down to my waist).

We're alright! We're okay! you panted loudly, as if not only trying to comfort me but to reassure yourself. Then you held on to me so tightly, I felt like I couldn't support you. Still holding me, you walked me over to the bed and just held me under you, as if you were shielding me from everything. If they come after us… If they come after us, you *Run*. Just run and run and run and run. And don't *ever* come back, you told me.

I couldn't leave you.

You started to cry, like your body was slowly chipping away, crumbling on top of me. Your chest heaved forward and back. Your breathing became my breathing. I kissed your tears and then licked them, your warm cheeks juxtaposing the salty cool as your tears meshed with the air. I kissed you gently. Your lips were puffy and your eyes were blood red. You coughed a little, letting out the phlegm at the back of your throat. Your breath was like an airbrush on my face.

No, you tried again. You listen to me. You leave me. You leave me the minute that they come, that anybody seems suspicious. You run and you save your own life. Do you understand? Don't worry about me. I'll be fine if you're fine. You pushed your leg in between mine, grabbing me and holding me still with your whole body, as it shook. You were so frightened. Your hands reached under my shirt, yearning for skin to prove to you the reality of my body underneath the clothes (the reality of Life underneath the Death, we faced).

I pushed you next to me on the bed. You just needed to lie down, for a moment. I put my head to your chest. I can hear your heart beating, I said, to reassure you that you were alive, too. We were almost sucked into the Machine. We escaped. We were alive. We've been through Hell and back, I whispered. And we're Alive. Shh… I tried to calm you.

I understand things, now, you said. But I thought that you had known, all along. And then you kissed me harder than you ever had. And you joined my body entirely, pushing every bit of skin together, holding us together like glue, until we were one Living Creature.

You whispered in my ear Kurt Vonnegut said *Here We Are, Trapped In The Amber Of The Moment. There Is No Why.*

…even when I'm dead…

Kisses, fragrant and soft (like flower petals against my skin) woke me, in the morning. Your eyes were still bloodshot, from the night. The bed sheets were wrinkled around your ankles. I wondered if you had slept, at all. You wondered how there would ever be a Happy Ending. But I told you, Every Tough Night has a Happy Morning. Every Tough Morning has an Easy Night. As long as I have you, as long as you are here and I am Thinking with you, Living with you, Talking with you, Being with you, then Beauty Isn't Dead. And Life is still worth living.

You moved my body close to yours and I slowly felt your soft lips against my skin.

Colors appeared that never existed before. We didn't even need to talk. Our eyes caught each embrace of communication. We gestured with our irises and conversed with our minds. Hope was still out there. You smiled and chuckled at me. And finally your lips parted (because you couldn't hold it in). Such A Romantic, you said. You made fun of me like you had the first night at the restaurant. So Serious. So Passionate. Rubbing your head against the pillow, your hair a mess, your lips spread wide across your face. And I love that, you whispered, too. You smirked in bliss, your mouth still and meditative. You looked at me, straight in the calming, soothing, crescent eyes of love. I love you. I love you…

I love you.

Kisses. Like none ever before experienced by the world, never before participated in so beautifully, so sweetly. Your thick lips sucked in mine and consumed them. You held me tighter, putting your arm around my back and placing my thigh around your leg. You touched my hips. You touched every part of me. Over and over, again. Relieved to see that all the parts were still there. That nothing was missing. You counted the number of toes, the number of fingers. You kissed each one gently, as if in prayer. Our naked bodies were warm in each other's glow.

Do you think this is what Heaven is like? you asked me.

I don't know, I told you. It really can't get much better.

You laughed and held me tighter.

I wish I could hold you so tight, I said. Whenever I try, you just show off your strength and hold me tighter. Will you hold me just as tightly when I'm old? Even when I'm dead? You can hold my Spirit, I said to you. You know me better than I know you. And I wish that I could know you. I feel like here, in this bed, I can know you as an equal. But what about out in that world? What will we say about each other? What will we do to each other, when one of us has our back turned? My thoughts rippled under the covers like a quiet breeze, slowly penetrating the natural curves of the fabric. My thoughts went in and out, fluctuating like the tide.

Shh… You covered my lips with your index finger. I will never turn my back on you. I listened to your words, meditatively focusing on each one, on the depth of their bond, the trust and weight of each syllable I will never turn my back on you. I will always be for you. I will save you countless times in countless lives. And we will always be together. I will *always* love you.

I will always love you, too.

...*enthusiasm in the daydream*...

Matt and Sarah invited us to an outdoor barbecue as they celebrated the installation of the new pool in the courtyard facing our apartment complex. Matt gave you a beer and told you Make yourself at home, no hard feelings over the weird commune suggestions to my wife and all that. Sarah tried to keep an eye on the kids as I traveled quickly in and out of her apartment, carrying trays filled with forks, knives, plastic plates, and everything else, watching twenty or so other tenants trying feverishly to make new acquaintances, distance themselves from the old ones, and remember the names of ones they had forgotten. It was sunny that Saturday afternoon. Not a cloud in the sky.

After I finished unloading what seemed like an endless array of trays and condiments, you waved me over to come sit with you and Matt as you shared that ever lasting beer in front of the glistening pool side.

So your boyfriend over here was telling us about how you're an artist, Matt started. And you blushed a little. As if you had revealed some Secret Identity of mine.

She never would have told you on her own, you explained. She's too modest.

…perhaps… I said. I tried to play the What If Game in my head. Perhaps Matt would have found out, sooner or later. Who knew? What if I told him tomorrow, instead?

He told me that you're a writer, Matt continued the conversation. You ever imagine yourself getting real famous?

Not really, I haven't been imagining, or dreaming rather, about my own future in a while.

Oh really? Matt questioned, finding this hard to believe.

Why not? Dreaming is what life's all about. That's why we go to the movies.

Even Horror Movies? I asked him.

Hell yeah, he took another slug of his beer and smiled, the droplets of alcohol glistening down his scruffy cheek. Those are called Nightmares.

Okay, I conceded. Since you know so much about The Importance Of Dreaming, what should I dream about? What should I want for the future?

Well (Matt decided to play with fantasies) let's say that you really did sell a whole lot of books… I guess you would have to write them first?

I guess, I joked.

Well, let's say you sold a ton of books. And then you became really famous. You wrote a Bestseller with a Cult Following. You know? Not some group of hoity-toity Intellectuals, but you really reached down into the very hearts and souls of some people way down. So, you touched these people. You connected with them. And then you decided to have a Book Signing. And at this Book Signing, you could only sign your initials. See? Because you were afraid of Identity Theft. That somebody might steal your signature and use it to buy things and get around to places. Well, that would be an awful mess. As you can imagine.

I can imagine, I answered.

Can you really steal an Identity through a *signature*? You pushed me gently with your shoulder as you took another sip of the beer.

Matt ignored you and continued in all seriousness. You have this Book Signing. And all of these people come. And you're sitting there. Signing your initials. And you decide to personalize each signed copy. So the first person you sign for is a Black Woman. With large, beautiful eyes. And you write in her copy I Like Your Eyes. And then the next person who comes is a man with a huge moustache and long sideburns and… and… a unibrow! And you decide that his personal note should say Nice Moustache. But then he reads the note and frowns and says But it was for my niece! And you say back to him, with the ego only a Bestselling Author could get away with Tell her to grow a moustache, then. I have high expectations. She has a lot to live up to.

What gall! I said.

What gall, indeed! Matt answered. And then, once you

become Really Famous, people that own these signed books will sell them on E-Bay for thousands of dollars. And people all around the world will read these strange personalized notes like Your Dog Smells Good and Where Did You Buy Your Coat?

Matt smiles when he sees my intrigued enthusiasm in the daydream.

And then you decide that you have nothing better to do with all of your money than send horrible revenge notes to all of your High School teachers that never thought that you would accomplish anything.

Don't forget Middle School and Elementary School teachers, as well, you chip in.

Thanks for that, I push you back.

Hey. No problem, you wink at me.

Oh yes! Yes! Matt continues, really getting into the story. So you send back these notes attached to copies of your novel. First to your Poetry Teacher that never thought you wrote poetry correctly. The one that said you only told stories and made you give all your poems bad titles. Then to your Music Teacher who never thought you would get anywhere in life with your attitude. Then! Then! Mrs. Marble!

I never had a Mrs. Marble, I tried to correct Matt.

Doesn't matter. You'll edit this later, he said, as if I were writing a novel right at that moment with my mind. So you send Mrs. Marble the longest note of them all. *You jealous bitch. You never thought that I could write so much and accomplish so much in so little amount of time. You're already sixty and you've only gotten one major work published. I have twenty and I'm not even thirty.* Yadda yadda yadda.

I sound awfully cruel, don't I? I asked you.

Yes. But this is just a Dream. Remember? you tried to reassure me.

Yes, yes, I say to myself.

Matt continued And then Mrs. Marble replies—

Sarah yelled from across the pool Peter! Peter! Somebody Help Me! He Tripped And Fell In! Somebody Help Me, Goddamn It!

Pete's small body had sunk to the bottom of the pool and was not coming up.

Oh God! yelled Matt. And he dived head first into the pool. His clothing quickly melted off of him like wax from a candle. Splashing like some gigantic sea monster, he touched the boy's frail, bluish body only to come back up to the surface again. He's Caught

On The Filter!

You jumped in. You jumped in so quickly (I've never seen you move so fast). One minute you were staring into my eyes, holding a beer, and the next you were splashing around that pool, just like a fish. And then (as the air became still for a moment) you splashed back out again with Pete's body. Pete's mouth was purple. You quickly put him onto the tile surrounding the pool.

Somebody Call Nine One One! yelled Sarah.

You put your mouth on his and you gave him artificial respiration. You pounded on his chest. And did it again and again. Turning him on his side so that he could spit the water out. Again, you breathed for him. I watched as in a moment the seemingly lifeless boy (motionless, still, and quiet) awoke and puked out the chlorine from his chest.

Sarah held Pete as only a mother could hold her son, his limp body shifting like putty in her arms. He was coughing violently and gasping. Thank you, whispered Sarah to you as she looked up, her clothing drenched in the boy's spit. Oh God thank you.

...shoes, shuffleboard, anything...

Pete was sitting on a towel, watching the serene surface of the pool. The gash on his forehead had been bandaged up by the local paramedics who arrived quickly to the scene after the most important moments were over. Pete's eyes were the same blue as the water.

The boy was knocked unconscious from the fall, explained the man in the blue uniform. Drowning would have been inevitable, had it not been for the strength of this man. He put his arm on your shoulder, but you drew it away (it seemed too heavy to lift).

Thank you, repeated Sarah. Over and over again. Holding the little boy's hand and watching Mary as her tear-stained dress moistened to a greater extent. Mary's dress no longer shifted in the wind but stood as stationary as her father.

Matt stood staring at the new pool he had installed. I should've made it into a Mini-Golf course. Or Horse Shoes. Shuffleboard. Anything. Why a pool, damn it? This was waiting to happen, Matt mumbled repeatedly under his breath.

The paramedics finally left. And you and I sat alone with the family for a little while outside, the pool motionless and undisturbed as tenants quickly shuffled inside their apartments (only to listen to the conversations going on outside from a safer angle).

Your son could have died, you said to Sarah.

I know that, she said. And I told you Thank You for saving his life.

Your son could have died like the thousands that are slaughtered every day, more willingly than he, through the Machines.

What are you trying to say? Are you insulting me after all of this? Sarah said. And Matt rose from his plastic pool side chair.

No, I told Matt, gently pressing his shoulder with my thumb and index finger. We're trying to open your eyes to something that is going on by relating it to something that has just happened. We're trying to explain to you that although *this* was just an accident, there are people who are willingly killing others in our neighborhood. Look how upset you were for one small child. You could always have another child. In fact, you do have another. That is what the government would tell you if you'd lost Pete to the Machine. They would tell you that you had another child. And they would encourage you to sacrifice her, too. We are saying that no one deserves to die, Sarah. No one! I walked over to Sarah and put my hand on her tightly closed fist.

Sarah shrugged a moment. Moved my hand from her tight grip. And said Get the fuck away from me.

Sarah. We're just... you tried to catch her before she stomped away.

You're just what? She turned. Telling me something I already know? Trying to turn my life experiences into some sort of metaphor for your Cause? Save it. I've heard it all before.

Sarah, stop! Matt called out to her. And she turned. One of her eyes gently releasing a never-ending supply of tears. Listen to them, he said to her. Just stop and listen. I can't take it anymore. This has to stop. This is Death. This is the Ever Present. And this is what it feels like. We can't ignore Death when it happens in our own backyard. Matt looked gently into her eyes, breaking the pleasant façade of their lives, sheltering their children from the real world. We can't ignore it, any more.

...it is not in heaven...

You know? Matt proposed to me over Instant Message, Sarah told me, sitting on her living room couch at ten o'clock that night, after putting Pete and Mary to bed. I realized this was the first time I'd really been invited into her apartment since I first moved in to the complex (other than just to grab silverware or to borrow some appliance). This was a real invitation. I realized how much more time I spent home since I was fired, since I was hunted down by a goon from the Death Machine Factory. You told me how you were getting to know Matt better, too. You were getting to know more people as people, making in-depth friendships now that you were home and unemployed. You no longer had the American Work Ethic pushing you to compete against others to make money. No. At home, we were all on the same playing field. It was like Capitalism took a nose dive in your personal life (not that Communism or Fascism was at the heart of it, either). There had to be something else out there.

It was lovely, Sarah went on, into little nostalgic details. She said We kept going back and forth. Paragraphs of Wireless Space. And then he asked me. And I said Yes. And she said We originally planned to go out that evening. To our favorite restaurant. Where we went on our first date. But it was raining... This was just so much easier. He even sent me music files of our favorite songs to serenade me during our conversation.

You pressed your ear close to mine as you leaned over the table to get your glass of water from a coaster. And you whispered in my ear I would never propose to you over the Internet. Or the phone, for that matter.

What are you whispering? Sarah said, upset that we should have any secrets from each other after living through that terrible circumstance. We're all friends. Just say it. She waited for a minute, her hands on her hips until finally she sighed and said Okay. So a proposal over the Internet may not seem that Romantic. But it was.

Did you meet over the Internet, too? you asked her rudely. I gently hit your arm to make you aware of your insult. And you said Hey!

Matt just put his hands on his lap and looked down at the floor, shaking his skull from side to side. Our lives were always obsessed with machines, Matt said with an empty groan, recognizing

95

how out of all of the moments of his life he had been. Out of all the Experiences, Lessons, Changes, and Revolutions he had lived through. That was the only statement that remained continuous and altruistic. It was somewhat pitiful and plain, like he had just come to terms with the tools of his life. We thought we were so advanced. So Advanced. We've regressed so much... He whimpered. His voice trailing off. He was a monkey with a computer, not a man with a mouth. We love them. We need them. We need them just to communicate the most basic, primal messages. Words that have been around since the beginning of Time. We need them now. He realized how having everything in terms of Technology did not mean that you had a fulfilled life. American Consumerism couldn't fill the voids in his Soul.

Maybe we always needed machinery, Sarah said, trying to explain. Like we always needed the Wheel. She played with her glass of water, leaning it gently sideways, watching the water flow back and forth like a seesaw. Then she gently put the glass back on the coaster on the coffee table.

Maybe, you said. Looking at me seriously, like a psychiatrist diagnosing a patient (or a mechanic after looking under the car, a surgeon after telling the family of some terminal illness). But should people sacrifice other people for our need for machines? What is more important? The number of people? Or the number of computers?

I once read about Artificial Intelligence, I told them, shifting the subject away from their nostalgia tied to machines. Programmers put it into some Video Games. The original intent was that machines could address disputes quickly, so that people don't have to worry and bicker about them so much. But machines are better at being Policemen than Judges. Unfortunately, the programmers found that although the machines could enforce the rules, they did not have the Morals, Capacity, or Disposition to make coherent judgments. People were required to do that. If people get too tied to machines, then they can't make rational judgments. And perhaps that's why the government decided to make a Death Machine...

Or maybe it's because things that happen in Video Game Worlds affect the Real World, you added (as if everything went back to one problem). Just as Life is affected by Art. So maybe if the majority of Video Games and the World Online is obsessed with carnage and bloodshed. Overall Anarchy. Maybe that determines how we govern.

It's not Art's fault, I interrupted you. Video Games and Art are just an expression of human emotion that already existed.

So, you continued. People are just so sick of order that they need brutality in order to endure the monotony of life. You made me think of the idea of Citizen Soldiers. Men expected to behave in Society and then sent off to War, told to kill people (by harnessing their animalistic instinct) and then brought back from War and told to conform to Civilized Business Suits, again. You made me think of people who didn't want to behave.

But maybe (you went on) if Society harnessed aggression into Society, it would make people fit into Society. Conform more. Make it easier for them to like life. Or be able to live with it. Things that happen in a Virtual World affect the Real World. (You looked at me). Especially Politics.

I think the Real World affects the Virtual, as well, I said, flipping your idea the other way around. It's an escape.

I imagined all those boys whom I grew up with. And how they were so socially awkward in Real Life, yet Online they could be anyone they wanted to be. A Warrior. A Hero. A Villain. A Creator. A Destructor. They could fall in love. They could have sex. They could die. They could be born again. They simulated the life that they didn't have and it made them feel good. Video Games let them release all of the pain of Reality. They escaped from a World Of Rules And Order that constantly forced them to act Socially Appropriately. And they went into a world where they could be entirely in control of their Identities (only to face the peril of some Fake Order).

Matt thought that our speculations were all well and good, but he wanted answers. How are we supposed to govern Peace if we can't even have Peace Online? How can we positively impact Reality through the Virtual?

Art impacts Life. Let's make Good Art. Let's make a Utopia. Online! I said.

People would enter it and screw it up like the Garden Of Eden. They would find out Secret Access Codes and destroy it, you said. Think about all of the pollution in the Real World. Well, just imagine that ten times quicker, Online. Because people are more advanced, now. People Online don't want Rules, Treaties, Peace, or Order. They want Chaos! And they want an escape from the ordinary.

I heard about a Video Game once that let people experience

true pleasure Online. But then would kill them in the end, Matt told you.

That's just some philosophy, you said. Nothing real. Man couldn't do that.

Man made a Death Machine, didn't he? I asked you.

It's true, Matt said. Someone told me it was true.

Who told you that was true? you asked skeptically.

It's as true as the Death Machine, I tell you!

Sarah shuddered in her seat. She rubbed her arms as though there was some sort of draft coming from the window behind her and no sweater would be able to stop the frigid ache as it crawled up her spine. Matt's legs crashed back and forth next to each other, as if they were going through some tidal storm, as though gravity had two platelets that were uneasily knocking into each other (like two awkward teenagers trying to make love, like a sporadic mental patient clapping his hands).

Enough! Enough! Matt called out. I hate Reality! I hate the Virtual! I hate Machines! I hate *hiding*! Can't we just come out into the open that we're pissed off with Society? With Man? With everything that's happened?

It is Man, yelled Mary. It's all Man's fault!

Hey! Wait there a minute! Man isn't inherently evil! you called out. Don't blame all of Man for this. We're people! We don't like this! Machines influenced us to do these horrible things. Have faith in Man.

Why have faith in Man? Sarah stopped you. Man created Machines.

Then in God, I said. Have faith in God. And that God will influence Man. You stared at me, annoyed that I disagreed with your humanism. There are some things (I stared you down like a long highway in the desert) that Man just doesn't have control over. There are things out of your and my hands. There are things beyond us. Things that we can't comprehend. There are things more Moral than our Laws, which we cannot perceive.

It Is Not In Heaven. You quoted Deuteronomy and I looked at you surprised. One thing I'll always give you is that you did know your quotations. You always knew the perfect words to put in at the right moments.

Not all of Man's actions are good, I said. Are you going to tell me that all of Man's actions are good? That all of his Morals are correct? That all of his Vandalism, Hate, Carnal Desires, Violence are always justified? That we should be ruled by the Primitive Leisure of a few men in power rather than by a more Natural Law?

Natural law! That's right! you interrupted me. Man Is Naturally Good.

Sarah and Matt stared at us, their heads shifting back and forth with the argument like a tennis match. We must have looked like an old married couple, our senile memories of philosophy spiraling around. I wondered if later that night Matt and Sarah thought that we fought like this every night in bed. How could we ever be together?

Man has evil inclinations, I said. Man does things that he thinks are Bad that he thinks are Good. There are Heavenly Actions in this world that make Good.

...true vengeance, true justice...

We tried everything we could. We tried to destroy every type of machine. From smashing in the windows of yellow Hummers to soaking laptops in boiling oil. Nothing would get rid of them. They kept popping up and reproducing like wild rabbits. So finally we gave in. We knew that Man needed his shiny things. His machinery.

We were walking outside a restaurant. It was so cold, but the snow was getting lighter. The air was misty and the tops of old cars in the parking lot were starting to rust.

You looked me and said I see you getting older.

I didn't understand. Was my hair getting grey? It must have been just the tint of the street light. It must have been the rays bouncing off my head from the moon. It wasn't me. It wasn't something that was wrong with me, internally. It wasn't that the coloring cells in the roots of my head were starting to die and lose their potential for turning a different color. It wasn't as if my skin was wrinkling, the groves and rhythms of it trying to keep up but gasping and losing time and space (gaining speed and then desperately stopping short, catching up with the rest of my skin, the melanin spreading, cells bumping into one another like racing horses and then collapsing on top of each other into one gigantic pile of skin). Wrinkles? No. I wasn't wrinkling. I wasn't pruning, as if I'd been trapped in a bathtub for years. My mind wasn't going. I was still as sharp as a tack. I wasn't fading, I wasn't delusional. You of all people knew. You knew that I wasn't going crazy, didn't you? Didn't you still believe in me? I didn't understand. My eyes shifting as I thought within myself. My feet shuffled me from one corner of the block to the next.

This whole experiment we've been doing, trying to expose the Machine from the inside, it isn't working. It's wearing on you.

You tried to make me understand. It was more than wearing on me. It was tearing me. It was ripping me. And it was shredding my head. Cutting my skin. Biting off my nails. Biting my lips. Making me bleed. It was like a mental disease that spread into every orifice of my cranium, burning neurons. Spreading. Then it was crawling under my skin. Pumping through my veins. I stared at the Gas Station across the street. I stared at the motorcycle rider, kicking his pedal, making a loud noise and then riding off into the darkness alone.

We started walking back towards the apartment complex. As we walked down the street, I saw a car dealership, (the giant American Flag, hovering, floating patriotically to and fro from the metal pole hoisting it at the pinnacle of American Modernity).

Man needs his machines, I told you, which was something that I had come to terms with (something that wasn't going away).

I started tearing and you said So?

So? I couldn't believe you were mocking right then. So, we're fucked. So we're all just meat for some insane Machine. And the worst part is that the government isn't even fooling us. They aren't even lying anymore about what the Machines are doing. It's not like *The Matrix,* where we live in some alternate reality and the Machines themselves are doing this without our knowledge. No! People are doing this to themselves. We are doing this to ourselves! And we're advertising it! And people love it! And they're volunteering! Because it's Sexy! Because it's just like another advertisement! We're all just being consumed by our own Consumerism!

It's not over yet, you said. I'm just saying… So what if we worship machines? So what if we're all so obsessed with machines?

We? Who put us into all of this? Why are you grouping yourself with them?

Because we're not perfect. We can't live without machines, either. A Breathing Machine. A Medical Heart Monitor. An Ambulance. We all need machines, today.

Machines! I spit on the ground and raised my hands up to the heavens. Why Machines?! I looked away from you and I started to walk more quickly.

Machines can save people. We could make Good Machines! We could make Moral Machines! Like Defibrillators. Like I.V. Machines... We could make... We could make a Life Machine to counter their Death Machine.

You tried to catch up with me.

What? I turned around a little bit.

A Life Machine. Create Life to make up for the Death produced from Machinocide.

Life? Human Life from a Machine? I tried to think about this ethically. Didn't you know that the Birth Rate decreases the more Society Advances? Didn't you know that that the government became so dependent on objects that it forgot about its people? Without people there was no power. There would be no people to have power over. The government needed people to govern. And they were running low. They forgot about their Number One Organic Material (more important than Fossil Fuel) living, thinking, acting, voting, human flesh. The Leaders needed Followers. Did the Followers really need Leaders?

Life Machine. Life Machine... I mulled it over in my mind. Bio Machine...

Well, we can come up with the name later.

Could this really be the answer? Could that just solve it all? I stopped walking for a moment. I looked at you and my irises dilated at your faint outline in the darkness. It was as if you sparkled.

Fight fire with fire. That's the only true vengeance, true justice for this world. An Eye For An Eye.

So we decided to make a Machine that would counter the Death Machine. A Life Machine. And you and I could have children. And you and I could raise them to live life and love life. And the world would be saved.

...mustard seeds...

What could we possibly do to stop it? Sarah asked you and me around my kitchen table.

Tell us what we can do to help, said Matt firmly.

We started slow. You had read somewhere that two scientists had won the Nobel Prize for their work in *Genetic Alteration*

With Disease Prevention And Treatment. I remembered our fingers gliding over the greasy shine of the magazine article in *Time.* I remember that we were in amazement, at first, unsure of what direction Science was going to take. Were people going to develop Genetic Diseases? Biological Weapons to further their human destruction? Or were scientists going to start countering the Death Of The World provoked by Globalization? Through the spread of Technology and Information, terrorist groups easily accessed information and the capabilities to do harm, the Media spreading the news of their actions. Could people possibly take the spread of Disease, Fear, and Death into their own hands? Could we start to provoke change? Instead of spreading information about Death, could we spread the word of Hope? Could we learn to create instead of destroy?

We had to start small. Plants, I told you. Let's start with Plants. We can research more and at a quicker pace. Morally, it will be less harmful. Especially when we are unsure of the exact answer. We can conduct more research, learning more about an area of Science that's blossoming.

The researchers that won the Nobel Prize were studying certain Plants. Tobacco. Lettuce. Tomatoes, you told me. And I think Mustard Seed. Yeah. Mustard Seed. You looked over the article, again. Latin Name: *Arabidopsis.*

Arabidopsis... hmn...

We wanted to genetically alter the birth rates of *Arabidopsis* plants to exceed their normal amount. Our goal was to Increase Life. We needed the resources and the environment for study. We couldn't work from our own kitchen. No one had the capabilities of a high-powered laboratory. So at night, we snuck into Biology Labs at local Universities.

It was broad daylight the first time we entered my alma mater. I used to work in the laboratories, so I knew where certain enzymes were kept and where the slides, test tubes, beakers, and chemicals were held. You made fake IDs with our names and pictures on them (saying that we were students). We looked like post-docs. We ran up the ten flights of stairs to get to the laboratories. A few people asked what we were doing there. You told them We've just moved here from a different lab. And we're here to learn more about your *Transgenic Plant Research In Reproduction* and eventually learn how it can be developed into Mammalian Breeding.

We're trying to expand our Intellectual Horizons, I said.

Later you would scold me for saying such a silly thing. But in some ways, it was very true. Intellect would help us change and save the future of humanity. Why couldn't I just tell them how I felt? The people in the labs smiled. They saw that we were quiet workers and every so often would ask about what we were doing.

We're trying to run a gel, but the machine isn't working, I said.

What do you mean? A red-headed woman asked.

Well look at our Negative Control versus our Vector Control, I stared at the fuzzy black lines at all different heights on the little piece of shiny plastic paper.

Maybe you just mixed it up, before the PCR.

Maybe. But, Jeez! I'm going to have to start over. I was annoyed that everything was so tedious, repetitive, and took so long. The redhead smiled and said that This is just how things are and things will get better once you get more results. It's all worth it in the end, don't worry. You're benefiting Science, after all. She was one of the researchers who worked late into the night. Weekends, too. Never ceasing. Never failing. Never faltering. She knew that there was so much work to be done. Never-Ending Work. And she believed in the higher purpose of it all. I didn't know how she could do it. How she could come in day after day, night after night, working sixty-hour weeks. It was crazy. Forty hours alone almost killed me. I never came home from work so exhausted, not even when I was working for the Machine. Being crouched over a lab desk for ten hours a day was much more mentally exhausting than checking paperwork for the Machine. Standing, tired, my eyes strained over microscopes, examining the embryos of *Arabidopsis* plants. I was surely losing my eyesight.

Hang in there, the redhead said as she walked down the hallway. It'll be alright in the end. Even if it seems like you are going to fail a million times, you're only getting close to the true answer.

But the disappointment of working for a month with barely any results was killing me.

A month is nothing, she told me as I labeled a slide in the back room. Tell me when you get to five years and then we'll talk.

Five Years. That astonished me.

I'm Madeline Price, she introduced herself. I'm the Head of the Plant Pathology Department at the University. She worked harder for better knowledge on the positive aspects of Science than anyone I'd ever met before. I watched her tiny hands as they gingerly spread across the tobacco leaves in the greenhouse. This is how you inject Tobacco Plants for UV Light Tests, she told me as she gently made an incision in the leaves with a razor blade. I watched the Plant start to bleed green juices and I was glad that I wasn't experimenting on Animals. These were only Plants. Plants that I would make sure did not get into the ecosystem until we were sure that they wouldn't hurt our natural food supply, only help it. I watched as Madeline took a water needle and injected (more like gently pushed) the fluid of her Transgenic Vector with Green Florescent Protein into the Plant. The liquid seeped through the Plant, creating a dark circle of leafy tones in front of our very eyes. You can see it right away, she told me. And I nodded my head. It was that simple to inject a Plant. It was that simple to study.

I started to study different types of Plants. I went from *Arabidopsis* to Tobacco to Corn to Tomatoes. As I read more and more about the evolution of these species, how they came closer and closer to the more complex Mammalian Gene System, I wanted to go further and further in the research. As I read more, I wanted to do more. I started experiments and I worked and worked, until all my results were successful and I got a smile and a Thumbs Up from Madeline as she folded up a large poster she had written to advertise a paper. This motion, from one colleague to another, was a simple recognition of all of the work that had unfolded around me. It made the panic attacks worth it. It made the sleepless nights, the painful awakenings, the dreams (those dreams full of day glow that just repeat the nightmares of reality and life over and over again) all worth it. Because I knew that this was truly the answer.

Even though things were going so well in the lab, our time together was not. Inconsistencies taunted me. One moment, life was full speed ahead, I was close to you, you were everywhere and we could sit down together as equals and nothing could have been better! Then there were those times when you weren't even there. When I never saw you. Those moments (the ups the downs) always happened at the same time. There was never a medium in-between the extremes. But you complained that there was never a span of time where I could be either with you or without you. I jumped ahead with my lab work and you were on the sidelines. That's when I started to have problems. Personal problems. Problems that Rich People talk to Psychiatrists about. Billionaires sit in their expensive leather chairs, whining and complaining about Work and Sex. Makes my life so picky and yet so general. I was just like a million other workaholics. And yet I was a very specific case. I knew something was wrong when specifics in our relationship floated away on craters to Mars and I was stuck thinking about you in terms of Generalized Morals rather than Personality. How our color scheme fits in with the rest of the world.

Don't you care what anyone else thinks about you? I asked you as you sat on the couch watching TV when I got home at eleven at night. Did you ever truly believe in me? Can anyone be so separate from a Community? From a Society? Can anyone really be an Individual on her own? I needed you and you needed me. And that was how the days pulled themselves together.

Madeline motivated me to continue conducting experiments. Keep working. Show the government and show the people that they are wrong, that they're going nowhere. She put her hand on my shoulder once in the laboratory. She looked down and then met my eye again. I believe in your Cause. I know that you're not a regular researcher. And that if the government knew what you were doing in this lab, you and I would both be imprisoned, she whispered. And then she dropped her hand and walked away.

Of course, the next week brought about continually negative results. Don't give up, you told me. I wished that outside it could have been snowing or raining, or something terribly upsetting that would have made everyone else's week miserable. But it was already August and it couldn't have been sunnier. Stop getting yourself down, you motivated me. Keep going. And when you get more positive results go public. Tell the masses.

Look at these numbers, I showed you in December.

This is a major improvement, you told me. This is really working.

On Plants anyway, I said.

So we'll expand it, you told me. We'll move on to other species. We'll move up the food chain.

You think that I should move on to more complex and developed forms of Plant Life?

Yes. You smiled at how I turned your words into a complex diagram for our future. Go for it, you urged me on. Madeline got me in touch with researchers at another campus lab. I created New Plants. New Flies. New Fish. New Rats. There were more Products and more Seeds.

...for Lucy's sake...

You were in the middle of dissecting a transgenic plant when they called us into the Main Research Library. The Head of the University Labs, Dr. Helen Reop, sat us down to tell us what they knew.

We know that you're not legally working here. We know that you've used thousands upon thousands of dollars in equipment for very advanced research, under our noses. I can't believe we were so oblivious. Even I thought you were both visiting researchers. How could I be so blind? How could our security falter so greatly?

I don't know, you said, estimating the improbabilities of what we had done.

There are a few reasons that we are not having you arrested right now, she continued. The first is that Madeline Price tells me that your research is an asset to the research of this Laboratory. The second is that we could use your research, good research, to promote this lab and receive more funding.

It's always just a numbers game, isn't it? I asked her.

No. Actually, it's also the fact that with more funding we can do better research and actually greatly advance Scientific Study on Crop Production. You were able to create Plants that can reproduce under the most extreme conditions. We can use this research with Plants and maybe just feed a few more million people and save this planet from widespread famine and starvation.

It was then that I realized that this lab (not unlike quite a few laboratories in the United States) was actually looking to improve this world, to leave a thumbprint that would shove humanity back in the right direction. Because they understood humanity's great Race To The Bottom. They understood Man's primal need to kill one another and destroy. Scientists understood Advancement to mean not a Mental Evolution, but a Moral Evolution and shift. To study how to make this world a better place in which people helped each other. If Man knew how to stop warfare, how to feed millions, Man would use it for Goodness. These were not the scientists who figured out how to make new Atomic Bombs or Biological Weaponry. These were the scientists that were disgusted by the politicians and decided to improve this world with or without their consent or policy changes. I wish you could have seen how my face changed, how my optimism changed in that flash of the moment. But you were too drawn to your own shocked smile (that crescent expression that cracked open on your face like an egg into a frying pan). It was organic. It was naturally beautiful.

We finally got permission from all of the Professors and Administrators to continue our study and to continue to expand it into Mammalian Molecular Biology. Neighboring scientists applauded our efforts. And soon we were speaking at National Forums, presenting our research in PowerPoint Presentations and on posters. We received fifty grants from private donors. Our research was published in Popular Journals read by the masses and Scientific Articles that only researchers in a particular field would have been interested in. Good Scientists (people with morals behind their brains) wanted us to change this country. And by God, we were going to do it.

We slowly went higher up the chain of Plant Life. You created Transgenic Farm Produce. Tomatoes. Lettuce. Corn. Every type of Plant Life was being depleted because we destroyed all of our farm land with urban growth (our rainforests with McDonald's cows). We could now make a small parcel of land yield seventy times what it normally produced.

We went to farmers named Ida and Lou Farr. We took a Greyhound bus out far from the city, the dust beating in through the windows. The air pushed in and out on my skin through the window slits, the sun barely beaming. You put your hand on mine in the seat and said to me Nice trip to the country, just the two of us. I laughed a little. You always made it seem like this was a big nothing. The really important thing was Us. Not the Journey. Not the Machine. Not what was Between Us. You have to understand that that was what had brought us together, in the first place. (That's what this story is supposed to be about).

When we arrived in Middleton, it seemed like the life had been sucked out of the soil. It was dry and your foot slipped against large clods of dirt. There was a Wal-Mart and a grocery store (some local chain that hadn't gone far but everyone in town knew the owners, intimately). We walked half a mile until we got to the Farr Farm, presided over by a small brown house. A little girl stood on the porch and waved to us. She ran into the house yelling They's here! They's here!

Go on inside the house now Lucy, said an overweight man in his mid to late thirties. Well, hi there. You must be the folks come to talk to me 'bout new types of seeds.

Yes sir, I said. And as we approached Lou Farr's porch, he smiled and shook our hands. This little one is my daughter Lucy. And my wife Ida.

Nice to meet you, we replied.

Lucy, honey. You go play in your room, okay? Ida told the child and she skipped off.

Ida and Lou sat down at one side of a large round wooden table that was cluttered with bank statements, newspapers, and late bill notices. You and I followed their example and sat on the opposite side of the table.

We'll be frank and to the point, Ida said. We're in debt over our heads. We can't make any payments because we can't make enough crops. There was a time when our farm and our neighbor's supplied the entirety of the nation with fresh produce. We don't have a huge amount of land and what we do have and what we produce isn't enough to sustain us when we have foreign competitors that don't care about the means by which they grow their product.

Now, what you're proposing we do is plant these new seeds...?

Just filling up a quarter of your land, you added.

And we're supposed to get Better Results? More Production Than The Rest Of Our Field?

In the same time it takes you to produce your other plants, you'll have seventy times the amount of crops.

And you studied this? You're not just coming in here without testing this, before hand?

We've tested it in Laboratories, you said added. The you added But not on ten acres of land.

I see. Lou looked at his wife. They were desperate. They needed anything they could get. If these were the Magic Beans that would bring the Giant, so be it. They just needed the Stalk. Something Green.

This is one fourth of our land we're talking about, Ida said. If this fails, we'll be screwed for sure. We'll have to sell everything. We'll have to go live with my sister in Minnesota.

What other choices do we have? We have to support ourselves. For Lucy's sake. Lou stared back at the hallway and saw two small hands clutching the doorway. Lucy, are you listening to our conversation? he called out.

Daddy? she said. Are we gonna lose the farm?

No, honey. We're going to be alright. Because these nice people have come to help us.

Okay, she answered.

You see then? said Ida. This *has* to work.

We handed them the Seeds for free. We told them to try it at first and that if they weren't satisfied they could just return the Seeds. Ida said that she would test the Seeds in the kitchen sink and then apply them to twenty acres of land. We didn't hear from them until two weeks later, when they told us to send more, because it had worked so well in the sink they wanted to apply the Seeds to the entirety of their plot. And their land prospered. They had enough money to pay off old loans. And enough to send their daughter to Private Undergraduate and Graduate School. More local farmers in the area bought our Seeds.

After a year, we distributed the Seeds to thousands of domestic farms. We had to charge a small price after a while, but the demand was great. We knew that there would never be a surplus and never be a need for them in the future. People would be clamoring from the roofs of their farm houses for years because of our work. Our produce tasted just as fresh and clean as any other fruits or vegetables without added preservatives. It had the exact same genetic makeup, except that its reproduction was enhanced to produce a greater amount of healthier produce. Yes. It was Genetically Altered. But it was altered to Preserve and Save Humanity's Future.

Soon, we had enough food to feed the millions of starving children in sub-Saharan Africa and Southeast Asia. And enough money to be able to ship it over to their shriveling bodies. I remembered when Sarah first showed me images of the starving children being fed, slowly. How they were slowly nursed back to health. I remembered the eyes of the farmers as they were given Seeds that would actually Survive and Produce well through the next harvest and through thousands of harvests after that, even though there had been countless years of drought. This would sustain them. I liked helping them become self-sufficient. After I had given them these resources, the people would be able to produce for themselves, they wouldn't need our overseas assistance, anymore. I liked to know they were sustaining long-lasting independence, not having to worry about paying back International Agencies or Federal Loans from thousands of miles away. Finally, they were in control of themselves from their own homes.

...then we'll talk higher life forms...

Madeline said we needed to Advance. We covered the Plant Life and our experiments with Fish were going well. We already repopulated the Tuna population off the coast of Japan. These Fish, differing from their ancestors, would be less susceptible to mercury poisoning. Our work with Mammalian Cells was taking longer. Government roadblocks were starting to arise. And we had to stall in the meantime as we waited for legislators to get over their own power.

Let's start covering Viruses. Bacteria, she said. We need to do *more* with our research.

I gazed into her calming eyes with slight uneasiness. I didn't know how I would feel about this. I understand Bacteria. Small Protozoa that I can poke at with my needles under my large microscope, I said. So small that I won't even feel they are there.

But other people will feel it's there. They will feel the impact of our research, it's so dire, you told me. And Madeline agreed, shaking her head profusely.

What about Mammals? I asked. The Machine is eating *People*. We have to counter *that*.

We can start to counter the Loss Of Human Life by stopping Diseases and Bacteria that have decimated Human Life, she answered.

But then it will come to Animals, won't it? you asked. I don't know how I would feel, dealing with the bleeding Animals, Dysfunctional Evolution, and Deformed Fetuses. We're talking about making people develop in strange new ways. Are you *ready* for that much change? Is the world?

Madeline once told me I would miss Science, if I left it. She said I would miss so much of it, that I would have to come back, whether I liked it or not. But I didn't start with Science. I started as an Artist. With Morals. You and I came from a world that had been warped. But we remembered it. You didn't know how to come to terms with things beyond your center, beyond the base of your experience, beyond what we had started with. What was I supposed to do? Give in totally, because I might eventually change within myself? As if it were all something beyond the original? Something unnatural? Could you roll with the punches? Or was this the weak spot? I had to find out for myself.

Start with the Bacteria, Viruses, and Protozoa, Madeline said. Then we'll talk Higher Life Forms.

In the end (you tried to urge me on gently) this is going to really help Mankind. Humanity needs you. Don't give up, now. There is so much more that you can do. That we can do. I need you.

...a delirious calm...

We worked on Bacteria Reproduction, so that we could recreate more and more Antibiotics and Vaccinations to send to those children dying in Africa. We created new strands of Vaccines so that Vaccine-Resistant types of disease wouldn't be able to completely decimate the population. On a windy morning, our private labs funded a medical team to drive up in deserted areas in big mechanical trucks. The engines roared down the deserted streets of over fifteen countries. We sent truck loads of these Anti-Viral Pills into Africa. A woman clutched her stomach, her unborn child cried with hope. She couldn't imagine who was providing the money to bring these trucks. Some strange people in white lab coats, maybe? But she was thankful. And she was happy. There was a positive growth rate in the Population and the Economy. The government no longer had to worry about paying off the debt attributed to the Weak Foreign Aid it had been receiving for the past century. It no longer had to worry about Imperialist Regimes feeding their people and then taking the money out of their back pockets. Those governments didn't want to be Like America. They didn't want to Develop. They didn't want to Westernize. They just wanted to Save Lives. And that's what we gave to them for free (and for the promise that they would never adapt or use the Death Machines in their countries). Their economies boomed and there was no lack of Energy, no lack of Natural Resources to get their Energy from. Our philanthropic machine had a reaction in the villages and in the cities. Soon, more and more people realized the free Health Care Benefit they could receive without any government sponsorship or back alley pay off. Whether the governments of some countries were controlled or collapsing, these people had the promise of a healthier Future, a healthier Present. People took advantage of what was given to them on a silver platter. People who refused to go to Clinics to be tested ran in droves when they found out that there was a Cure. At first, people came pushing and shoving, sweat dripping down their necks as they desperately heaved their children to the front of lines. Then suddenly, when the few Doctors in Clinics explained that there was enough for everyone, for Everyone and for Their Children and for Their Grandchildren, people settled into a delirious calm. It was like walking into Utopia. It was like the scene in *The Wizard of Oz* as Dorothy walks from a dreary black and white into a colorful landscape. It was like walking into a new type of Heaven they could only dream about. They saw Color and Justice for the first time.

I watched on TV as millions of people who would have died within a year were saved. My television went from black and white to color. The Boob Tube, the Gore Box went from the news being Dreadfully Depressing to Uplifting to Beautiful to Respectful. It was as if for a moment in Human History, things went from Pessimistic to Optimistic. Life never seemed so ever-present. So Idolized. Revered. Worshiped. Adored. Admired. Life was precious, again. And that sacred idea was restored, once again.

You saw the Anchor People's faces on the news, how light seemed to shine ever more brightly on their faces, as if they thought to themselves while reading the cue cards Finally Something Worth Reporting. Something Giving My Life Meaning. That I Live In A World Where This Sort Of News Is Possible. That I Am So Lucky That I Get The Pleasure Of Reporting It. It looked like honey dripped from their chapped lips. They could taste it. Things were *changing*. Finally, things were actually Progressing.

There was still some news coverage attacking us. People claimed that because of the widespread use of our treatment, new Bacteria and Viruses would show up that were Resistant. They spoke about how America was over-Medicated. That people took prescriptions even when they didn't need to. They took Antibiotic Prescriptions when they had Viral Colds (and so forth). Others asked *Over-Medicated? Or Just Medicated Wrongly?* claiming that *We Need To Prescribe The Right Drugs For The Right Illnesses* and that even then *There Will Be Drug-Resistant Strains Of The Same Diseases*. In response, we made even more new Vaccinations that infectious agents wouldn't be resistant to. We made different varieties of Vaccinations for Diseases that hadn't been active for centuries (and would never be, again). We made Vaccines to fight strains of Bacteria and Viruses that didn't exist, yet.

Why are they doing all this foreign aid and they can't do anything for Americans, at home? Globalization may be good for everyone else, but it's not good for us at home! a woman cried out on *Oprah*.

We weren't encouraging Globalization. We were just using it because it was there and it wasn't going away. No one was going to stop it. We had to use the technology at our finger tips, so we continued producing medicine until we had enough to give to the poor people living in the Unites States, too.

...*connections*...

We need to start talking about Mammals, Madeline told you and me. I was ready for this talk. I braced myself. This is still under the radar, Madeline began. Legislation hasn't passed entirely in our favor. Start low, again. Simple Mammals. Rats and cats. And then we'll talk larger Animals. Eventually, you will have to start working with dairy farmers, meat packing plants, the whole shmigeggie. Your research will become Mainstream. It will have a huge impact on the Food Industry. It will be Positive. It will change things for the better. It will change Globalization. More Domestic Production than International Importation. It will decrease Global Warming. You can do it all. But it's still not getting to the heart of what the Machine is after. The Machine isn't after cows or fish. The Machine after People. She paused for a moment to let us reflect on how far we've come. After you've gone further with Mammals, I'll get you in touch with some top scientists, who will talk about working with basic Primates. And then you will need to start working with Humans.

Humans? People? Recreate how *People* are mass produced? you questioned in shock, as if this hadn't been in your mind before.

It's what has got to be done to counter the bloodshed. We don't need deadly energy from people, anymore. We have to prove it to them. We have to recreate *Life*, Madeline told us.

I think we need to finish our work with Amphibians and other life forms before we get into Humans, you said.

Alright, I said. Let's try.

Next we mass produced Animals, especially those species which were becoming extinct because of Global Warming and (you guessed it) Globalization and Urbanization, so that Biodiversity would be preserved. Birds. Birds that no one had seen in decades because they were so rare, their beautiful feathers multiplying in crazy huge numbers like spores on a moldy piece of bread. I watched as old species renewed slithered across the far bounds of the earth, to places that had disappeared. Animals regained control. Those Diseases (you heard about them, they fester off of new species of bugs and beetles on trees) became obsolete now, because we had enough of those endangered species to eat the bugs, to kill the Diseases. There were more healthy trees, as a result.

We started with Birds, Fish, and Amphibians. We met with Zoologists to help us determine which Animals needed to be reproduced the most and in what numbers. We needed to know the proportion of different species, so we didn't completely mess up the Natural Order.

Then we worked on Mammals. This took a long time, because the government did not want us working with Embryos and Sperm. A man from the Department Of Homeland Security came to check out our lab. His name was Richard Finn and he stood five feet, eleven inches tall in a navy blue suit with an American Flag button pinned to it. He carried a black briefcase and must have been in his mid to late Forties. He had a unibrow. He had perfect posture, but a mouth that curled and drooped into a frown. The lines on his forehead were ridged and deeply defined. Richard Finn liked the sound of his expensive shoes tapping on the linoleum floors of our laboratory.

We sat him at a big round table. We thought it would remind him of King Arthur's Court (or more currently, the War Room in the White House). This was a War. We weren't going to stop what we were doing. They would use Force and we would use Peace. Something would happen in the end. Some outcome would be there. We wanted him to sweat in his expensive suit. We wanted him to go home with sweat stains in his shirt that he would see in the mirror as he took off his jacket. We wanted him to have a shocked realization of the state of his own fear. And we wanted him to look curiously at the stain that would be left from his blue suit onto his white skin. We wanted him to look at himself like some Creature From The Black Lagoon had just emerged from that suit, his scale covered skin exposed to the florescent lighting of his bedroom. We wanted his wife to stare at him in disgust. But wait. This was how the whole argument began:

Mr. Finn began a little nervously with Obviously your research is having a large impact on our Society and our government. The government would like to endorse and buy your technology from you, in order to better supply it to the People At Large.

I think we've done a pretty damn good job already of

supplying it to the people that need it, you chuckled.

There's been word that you are developing a machine that will revolutionize how Mammals and very probably People reproduce. Mr. Finn shifted his eyebrow.

Did you hear that? I said to you. There are Science Spies even in our own Laboratory.

Look. This technology is very important. It will have a huge impact on the world. The government has to monitor it... He wanted to get through to us so desperately he didn't know what else to say. It's like the A-Bomb for Christ's sake!

Except that Atomic Bombs kill people, I said.

They still kill people, around the world, you added. Haven't done a very good job with that technology, now have you?

Look. There is an urgent need for the government to be able to regulate this type of technology. And we would appreciate your cooperation.

You mean shut it down? you questioned his motives. We know the government can't monopolize this type of technology unless legislation from Congress is passed. And with its increasing popularity...

On the front page of the paper today (I picked it up) *Five Hundred Thousand Saved In Botswana.*

I don't think any legislature is going to attack the desires of its constituents, you said.

I can guarantee you that there will be legislation on the subject, whether you like it or not, he added. Life should be put in the hands of those in charge.

You mean like the Machine, you said. You mean like legislation attacking Abortion? You mean like Euthanasia? Or perhaps you're referring to the Death Penalty? I don't see how government ownership made anything more Just. If anything, it made it much more Severe.

The government needs to supervise people's Rights And Technology. That's the only way to put it.

It seemed like his beliefs were starting to come out. His face started to turn red. Rougir... Like reddening. He was reddening like a tomato.

Oh, and you've done such a swell job so far, I said sarcastically, getting up from the table. I felt a little queasy. An old memory sat in my stomach like too much candy on Halloween. I felt uncomfortable sitting at the same table as a representative of the government that killed John. I needed to fiddle with something, to get my hands busy. Why is it we always do something so arbitrary when something important is being discussed?

Can I be frank, Mr. Finn? I don't see any government officials ending their lives through the Death Machine. It seems like they aren't Patriotic enough to give back to their country in that way, you said to him.

Like the War! I called out, getting myself a cup of coffee as I took a break from looking under a microscope all day.

So we're just out to help the people who are considering that option. And not the government.

You shook off Government Finances, Government Grants, and Government Supervision like a dog desperately trying to free himself of flees. At least you didn't scratch yourself. So Mr. Finn left us. The government did not support us. However, Private Organizations were more than willing to donate all that we needed to continue our study.

We figured out how to make an Artificial Womb. Its texture was more durable yet lighter in weight than the average Mammal's. And I remembered gazing at the first one that we created that we produced in a body. It was so pink. It was like all that talk about how the birth canal was misshaped for proper, safe births, had been corrected by humans. It made everything so much easier. With this, no Caesarians, no Stillbirths. Everything would be alright. It was a new playing field for studying Genetic Diseases like Down Syndrome and Tay Sachs.

We also started curing different types of Cancer (I know, could you believe it?). Diseases that were around since the ancient Greeks. Things that no one ever thought humans would be able to cure were cured. Those Supposed Causes (the plastic bottles in the refrigerators, excess coffee, too much milk) were not the Causes, at all. It turned out that the Western view that everything should be in moderation was not the correct way. I was glad that I was there to figure out that many of our Scientific beliefs were wrong. I was glad that I was not just continuing it, not just blindly exacerbating the problem. When I was little, I always imagined that if I ever became a Scientist (a famous one, like Dr. DiGennero, who did so much and got put in all of the text books) that even after my death I would be exalted by the Medical and Scientific Communities. That decades later, Scientists in a more advanced age would prove all of my theorems wrong. That they would find that all that work I had done, although it had some good points, was really some pathetic, simplistic minor study, that used uncontrolled variables that Scientists had all found were Carcinogens. What if I was Marie Curie and I was touching radioactive material all day with my bare hands? What if they had to put my lab notebook behind a protective glass covering, because it was dangerous to other humans? Or worse, that I had actually hurt Humanity through my study? Regressing information, instead of making this world better? How long would it take for them to know that my research was worthless?

I don't know if it's Art or if it's Morals or if it's Science that's going to save this world, in the end (in a million years to come when this problem comes up, again). Maybe it's just a mixture of all of them. I think people need all of them to live. To be Successful. To be Happy. Or rather, just to be Fulfilled. Maybe it's more than that. Maybe it's talking to you. Maybe it's like what Martin Buber said, that it's really all about Relationships, that how we treat one another is the most important thing in the world. I don't know if it's Reason or Intuition or if it's Distrustful Cynicism or Blind Faith. I think it just has to be both or in between. Sometimes in philosophy text books there will be Spectrums. Throw the Spectrum out the window. It's not about one or the other. It's about them all. There are small dosages of everything in everything else. Everything is connected. It's about connection.

Connection.

Madeline told me something once, about a time when she was in College. It went like this:

It was eleven twenty-four PM and I was standing outside of Fred's room. You'll never meet Fred. He was part of my life for such a brief time, like all those adolescent crushes that slowly dissolve from your memory. First, you forget their voices. Then their names. Then their faces. Then their existences. You don't remember that boy who sang to you in front of a crowd. Or that boy who gave you the flu. Or even that boy who drew your face in the moonlight. No. They are gone. They dissolve into generalizations you will tell your friends and teach to your children when they want to know about you and what you were like when you were young.

Anyway, I was knocking at his door. And then I heard it. It was faint yet distinct. It wasn't something I was just making up in my head. There was definitely a noise. Definitely a voice. A *female* voice. I heard it and then I heard Fred respond to it. They were talking in his room. And I knew that he didn't hear my knock. And I knew that knocking was futile, because no matter how loudly I banged on that shoe-stomped-blackened dorm room door, I will never be able to interrupt what they had. Their *connection*.

And suddenly I remembered all of the connections that I destroyed in order to get to this point. In order to be waiting outside of his door. Listening to him talk to another girl. Probably his next girlfriend. I remembered Lisa. I remembered how *she* was the one with the big crush and how she came into my room and sighed and moaned and told me about how much she loved this guy, about how she wanted so desperately to be more than his friend. How he asked her if he should break up with his girlfriend in order to Explore Other Options. And how Lisa thought that that meant her. Her in his bed. Her being his girlfriend. Not me.

It started with Salsa Dancing. You see, I sent Fred a Text Message and he never answered it. I asked him to take free Salsa Dancing Lessons with me and a few friends. No. He didn't show up. And the dancing instructor immediately had the boys and the girls pair up. No. I didn't have a partner. Most girls didn't have partners. So I was standing there alone. With nothing to do but watch the other partners and their *connections*.

Then, as my friend Lisa convinced me to leave because we didn't have partners, I passed by my friend Paul outside. He was going somewhere. I said a quick Hi, but I didn't ask where he was going. I didn't try to *connect*. Instead, I thought of knocking on Fred's room and seeing if he was around. Lisa and I talked for a while. I felt guilty leaving my friend Julie back at the Salsa Dancing place. But later, Julie returned and said she had fun. So it's not like I totally ruptured *that connection*.

Lisa called her friend Kate. Kate was watching *Rent* with friends. You wanna come? Again, I thought of Fred. No, I think I'm going to pass. I'm not a big *Rent* fan. I think it's kinda hokey. Yeah, me too, she retorted and was off to go see her friends. And then I left you back in my current predicament, waiting outside his door and knowing that I would never be inside.

So maybe I exaggerated. Maybe I didn't destroy every friendship in order to waste time on some guy. I certainly didn't lose the opportunity to tell you this now, did I? Of course, all the names have been changed and years from now no one will remember and Fred won't even know what happened. It was a shame he lived in my building. I had to deal with seeing him for the rest of that year. You know? He didn't even like the Beatles. Who doesn't like the Beatles, for heaven's sake? What a weirdo. Okay, so calling Fred (who I freak danced with one night at a club he invited me to) a jerk doesn't really make me feel any better. But telling you this, years later and getting out my feelings and realizing that things that I think are a big deal really aren't a big deal after all, makes me feel better. Believe it or not, I did make friends later that year. I didn't even have to talk to the random man eyeing me at the Metro Station as I got off to make my (yes, you guessed it) *connection.*

Is it strange to say that I am relieved that that relationship didn't work out? Because I started classes a few days later and I didn't want to have to deal with my fantasies during class time. I don't think there ever is an ideal *time* for a relationship. Not in my life, anyway. There certainly haven't been ideal *relationships.* I'm not the type of woman that randomly hooks up with every guy on the street. And in most of my relationships, I never get to know the guy well enough in the first place so I find out later that the guy I'm going out with is a real jerk. Before a relationship, I usually over-analyze everything to the tee. Every serious conversation and move we will ever make, so it's like I've already lived through the entire relationship without him ever having to be in it.

I was not crazy you know? Just because I was eighteen-years-old and I was not ready to lose my virginity or get raped at a party did not make me crazy. I don't think anyone is really ever ready for some things. I wasn't ready for my father's death. But that wasn't a shock and blow. Everyone always talks about mourning as being a Blow. Usually people associate a Blow job with Pleasure or Blowing up a balloon or even Blowing bubbles. I've never seen death as anything to do with Blowing. For me, it's always been a slow, painful shot. Like the one you get for the measles, which you can feel for the rest of the day, sliding down your arm and making your whole body cold and numb.

Is that my problem? Am I frigid because of pain in my life? Bullshit, ha! What a *connection*!

I felt so empty. And I know you hear this story and you're hoping that for once a person will take the road less traveled and try to tell you an uplifting tale that will set your spirits on high instead of a depressing one like this. But let's just face it, My Story, My Life Right Now, is depressing. I think of Fred alone with that girl in his room. I think of him with his allergies and telling all the people in his hall that he went out with Some Girl (being me) From The Building Last Night. People asked me how the party was. I said Great. I had a shitty time, other than rubbing my vagina on Fred's thigh. He said he wanted to dance more with me. I stopped thinking he was attractive the minute he told me that his puke was green after margaritas and that's why he never drank them any more. I stopped thinking he was attractive when he waved a purple tongue in my face and told me it was from having a ton of wine and I thought to myself From A Box?

I don't think that I did anything wrong. No. I didn't hook up with him. I had to go home, because I had to get up early. And I couldn't stand him leaving me for fifteen minutes at a time so he could go do *Something Else* with *Someone Else* and then come back to dance with me. I'm a One Woman One Man type of person. I don't do *ménage-a-trois*. And more realistically, I just don't want to be a heartbreaker. I don't want to break up some guy and his girlfriend. I don't want to be the bitch that destroyed their *connection*.

Even this I over analyze! Maybe I should be a philosopher and just think about life all day long. But I would need a way to express it! So I'm going to tell you this wonderful story. About Life. And yes, you will make the same mistakes. But now you can know what those mistakes will mean. And maybe, just maybe, you'll realize they weren't mistakes, in the first place. They were just Lessons In Life. I like the fact that through these episodes I came even closer to understanding who I really am. I was uncomfortable all day today because I kept imagining that I would end up hooking up with some guy I met only two days ago. *I was uncomfortable.* Why couldn't I just listen to myself? Thank God that Fred's got some girl in his room. Thank God that this whole shenanigan isn't going to work out. Because I didn't want it to work out. I didn't want to do it. Because that's just not the type of person that I am. I guess this experience brought me some insight into myself. I made my own personal *connection*. I *connected* to my True Self.

Madeline, I said. Look at all that you've accomplished over this time! How can you be so insecure about things in the Past? How can it haunt you, when you have so many new, good memories for the Present and the Future? I asked her, but she just shook her head and kept her eyes shut close to a sliver. I wondered if she was about to cry. She walked away from me, upset that I didn't understand her raving. I got up and followed her, putting my hand on her shoulder as a close friend who cared for another friend. I was worried. I wish that I could have empathized with her more, that I could have consoled her more than I actually did. I tried. I desperately tried. But it didn't work, I guess. Some people aren't totally whole, even when it seems like they should be on top of the world. I think that Madeline will be alright. I know that she is alright, now. She is fighting with us for something that she loves. She might have been alone (or merely seemed alone) but she wasn't. She had me as a friend. She had a Cause to motivate her.

I feel alone sometimes, too, I told her.

But how can you feel alone? You have some guy with his arms around you. Someone to hold you tight at night.

It's not about him. This is about me. This is about me trying to come to terms with who I am. It's about how we treat each other, but it's about how I think and I act, too. It's not like the minute you have a boyfriend everything is perfect. Or suddenly you can read people's thoughts. Or suddenly everything in the world that was hurt and broken is repaired. No. If anything, it's the opposite. Now you have someone with you to witness all those glasses shattering, all those painful things happening. It doesn't make them go away. It's just putting someone else, someone foreign and unfamiliar, right in the middle of it. Making them smell it. Touch it. Lick it. It puts them in the center of every bit of life that pinches your skin and clings to you like a wet bathing suit. It's exposing them to harmful chemicals. It's second-hand smoke.

I don't understand, she told me.

I don't know how to explain this, but he doesn't determine my Fate. I do. I have to decide what I want to do with my life. This isn't a Compromise Situation, like I signed my life away on some slippery coated contract. No. This is Me. With Someone Else. And we're both doggy paddling, trying to stay above the surface in the deep end... or even just in the kiddy pool. It's an Endurance Test. We have to keep up, somehow. We have to keep paddling. And we have to keep breathing. And it's hard. It's really difficult to keep afloat. To keep breathing. You end up coming out of things, gasping for air.

Madeline's blank eyes stared me down. She was curious. She was intense and she desperately wanted to know how it felt. I wish she knew, too. Then I could share more experiences. We could reflect and bond in a new way. A Shared Existence. But that wasn't happening.

When this is over, Madeline stared at me I'm going to find out who I really am.

Haven't you already found that along the way?

Maybe, she said to me. Maybe.

Madeline walked down the Science Laboratory Hallway. She stood quietly for a minute and looked back at me. You're really an amazing person, she told me. I blushed.

...the third one...

Take a look at this, you said, stooping over the large black microscope, adjusting the lenses to the image on the large screen next to it. You showed me the glistening mutated Stem Cells on the screen. We'd been studying these for a while now, monitoring their development inside the Mammalian Subjects. It was confirmed now. I've made them into liver cells.

I put my arms around you and I felt the air press out of your lungs, the pressure release like the loosening of a belt strap (like the opening of a champagne bottle). You kissed me slowly, as if your discovery coincided with some anniversary of our relationship. As if our lives were so interconnected and tied down to the Cause.

There is a belief in Judaism, you know (you started to tell me) that there are three kinds of relationships. The first is the relationship just based on Things. Materialism. There is a lot of love today that is based on that. The second is a relationship in which the two partners are focused solely on each other. They screen everything out in the world and selfishly only think about one another.

What is the third? I asked, curious, drawing away from your cheek.

A relationship in which the two people love each other, but they focus on issues beyond themselves. They serve the world together. They save the world together.

We do that, I kissed you. The Third One. We're the third one.

The third one is the best one. It's the Holiest one.

But marriage? I asked. Isn't it only Holy if we're married?

You stared down gently at the research. You weren't concentrating on its complex specifics. Instead, you focused on its general idea. You thought about the concept of our relationship and our research and our lives together, our commitment to an issue and to each other.

I don't know what that means, I said.

You lifted my arms from over your head. Yes you do. Don't say that you don't. You do. You do know what it means.

But...

You've been acting innocent and ignorant since this whole thing began. Or at least since we got serious about creating a Life Machine. Because it would permanently put us together.

What? I don't...

Yes. You do, you said. You don't want that do you? You don't what that, do you?

What?

You turned around and yelled Marry me, damn it!

I backed away from you. Oh... oh... I... I can't.

This is what I'm talking about, you pointed towards me and chuckled evilly. Goddamn it! It's like everything with you! I tell you that I love you! I tell you that we're doing a great job! That we're really fighting something Evil! And then you back down on me. It's like you just don't believe in yourself. It's like you're afraid of something. Like you're scared of Life. Of your own Destiny. But tell me. What is it? What Are You So Goddamn Afraid Of?

Everything, I told you honestly. I'm afraid of growing up. Of making definite conscious decisions. Of messing up. Of making mistakes. Of having to deal with regret. Of guilt from lost dreams. Even worthless dreams, as they may sometimes seem to some people.

Do they seem worthless to you?

When we were working in the Factory, it seemed like Yes. We were not doing anything productive, but learning more about the Evil inside of this *thing.*

Alright (you must have felt a hot lump of lament rise in your stomach).

Most of all, I'm afraid of not accomplishing anything. Of not winning in the end... Of losing you.

You are going to lose me if you don't marry me, damn it! You paused. You could tell that that wasn't working. That I didn't believe that I would lose you that way. Over some argument. Some disagreement over a piece of paper. You've already accomplished so much. Why do you beat yourself up like this?

Because I'm the only one that really can. I'm the one that gets to me the most. I'm the one who has to. I have to beat down my own ego.

Or just your Happiness? Are you just beating down emotion?

You were silent and you looked away from me. You did

really love me. You truly did, didn't you? I could feel it from the nervousness in your rising shoulders and the way you shuffled your feet. I could feel it like a heart beat or a lightning cloud over my body.

What is it going to take? you shifted your argument. Tell me? This is it. This is me in love with you and wanting to make it permanent. And you won't even give me the time of day. You looked at the wall and then back at me, something malicious in your eye. It's John, isn't it? It's John. Goddamn it! That's why you won't marry me. He's dead! He's fucking gone! Damn it!

This isn't about John!

Then what is it? Just tell me...

You started to get up from the seat and come toward me. I backed away, again. Unsure of wanting you to touch me. Not after you just said that to me. Not after blaming my lack of commitment to you on John.

It hurts when you talk to me like this. When you treat me like this. When you blame him for how I am. I was always like this. I was always like this with you. I would have been this way even if I met you before him. Don't you understand that?

You looked down for a moment. But it hurts me, too. It hurts so much. You looked away from me and walked toward the wall. I stared at your back. It was curved and hunched over and you did not look back at me. This is how it would be, if we just ended it then. I could imagine you hunched over. Forever. I could imagine myself looking only at your back. Never seeing your face, again. As you walked farther away, I walked toward the microscope you were just looking through. I looked at the Genetically Altered Cells and how they had developed so perfectly, without a scar in the world. It was perfect. It was beautiful and untouched, with so much potential. And I looked back at you. Because I wanted you to see it too.

Could you rebuild Dead Tissue?

...people danced in the sand...

The street lights reflected against the rain on the bus window like glistening computer screen lights from a failing Nineteen Eighties video game. Red, yellow, and white lights glittered against the long dark paths of the street. We were getting back to the apartment complex late, after the seminar we held discussing our research. I stared blankly out the window.

Everyone kept asking if we were married, you put your mouth close to my ear, to make sure that I would hear you beyond the buzz of the bus. You didn't want to yell at me, any more. I didn't respond. I just looked at the people running in the rain, their blurry outlines barely distinguishable from the massive smeared landscape of buildings.

No one asked if we were married, I turned over to you, my eyes near your lips. It's all in your mind.

Alright, you smirked. So maybe I wanted them to ask if we were married.

They asked if we were together, I told you.

They did? What did you say?

I said we were, I told you and turned my head back toward the buildings outside. The grant money should help for our research with Cancer. We'll need the backup money to order the Infected Tissue from MIT.

Tumors... We could fight Tumors. We did it in Plants. We fought the Tumor Mosaic Virus in Tobacco.

We did, I agreed.

Retroviruses, you said. What an amazing concept. Who knew that the application of new DNA to the cells... you drifted off.

Yep. I was still focused on the people running, covering their heads with newspapers and ducking for cover under large overhangs on the sidewalk.

I'm glad, you held my hand and gripped it tightly so that I turned toward you. I'm glad that I worked on Stem Cell Research with you. That we found out how to regenerate lost or damaged tissue so that people born with only one kidney or one lung could grow another and survive for a much longer time, together.

I turned toward you and looked you straight in the eye. I am glad, too. I looked down at your lips. You licked them and then I kissed you. You looked back at me as I slumped down in the seat. Rain always makes me tired.

Will you marry me now? you asked me.

What would our wedding be like? I asked you.

I would wear a white tuxedo. And you would carry some sort of flowers...

I want to get married at the beach. Near my parents' house. I miss it there. There is a spot where I saw a wedding, once. People danced in the sand.

Did people go swimming? Did people just leap into the water? I could imagine just wanting to jump in the water, when you're so close.

When you're used to living so close to the ocean, you don't really feel the urge to immediately go swimming, any more. Your urges, your love for it dies down.

Oh, you said.

But we can go swimming, if you really want to. Does that mean I have to wear a bathing suit under my dress?

...So... That's a yes? Your eyes widened.

I kissed you. Do you want to know why I wouldn't marry you, now?

Yes. You did desperately want to know.

I really, really, really... And I'm not lying when I tell you this, I digressed.

Just tell me, you said.

Alright. Okay. When I was in college, I used to know a very religious boy, who thought that any sex before marriage was a Sin. And that people would go to Hell if they did that. He saw that I was dating someone. And I heard him talking about me once to a friend. And he said There goes that Whore Of Babylon.

What? you asked me. What does that have to do with anything?

I'm getting to that, I continued. So this boy called me the Whore Of Babylon. And I got very upset. And he said that I needed To Get God Back Into My Life. As if I had somehow lost something Holy. He called me Unholy. Well, it turned out that the whole time that I was dating this other guy, the religious guy just wanted to get in my pants.

What?

This boy was jealous. He just wanted to date me. And so he tried to make me feel guilty about dating the other boy. When you said that it was only Holy if we were married, I wanted to make sure it wasn't because you thought that I was Unholy. Or that we were Unholy now. The way we are. Practically living together. If we're not Holy, now, why would we be Holy later? It isn't about being Holy. It's about doing something good for the world. I kissed you again and my eyes got tearing. Don't you understand? We were always Holy. No matter what we did in our Past with other people. It doesn't matter.

Do you believe in God?

Of course I do. I don't think that Man controls everything. There's got to be something else out there. It's Nature. It's Everything. We just have to make room for things that we can't control. Like Global Warming.

You laughed. Like Global Warming? So you do want God to come back into your life.

Not just mine. God's never been gone from mine. I can't explain. It's not like I want to convert any one. I don't want to proselytize. I just want to make Man have a little more Humility. Man can't control *everything*. Man has to leave room for Fate. For something beyond Modernity. Beyond Globalization and Technology.

Do you love me because I believe in something beyond technology?

Maybe. Do you believe in something beyond technology?

And that's when you totally surprised me.

I believe in Man, you said. I couldn't believe it. I couldn't believe that you had come out of all of this as a Humanist. I believe in Man's Ability, Man's Capacity To Do Good Above All Evil Inclinations.

Suddenly, our bus ride had turned out to be a philosophy discussion. There's got to be something beyond Man, I told you.

I hope, you said. But I don't think you were sure.

...someplace private and calm...

Our concept of using Retroviruses to counter Cancer and Viral Diseases soon became a Medical Norm in Hospitals around the country. And then around the world. Our practices in Cell Regeneration saved millions of lives.

During our trip to Asia, you stopped me in a hallway as we walked from air terminal to air terminal Will you marry me, now? You became more insistent.

Do we have to talk about this, right now? I kept walking, luggage still in hand. I was in a rush. I didn't want to talk about this. I had already been serious all day. Do you remember when you used to be fun, and make me happy and not pressure me about these types of things? What happened to the guy that did that? Huh? What happened to him?

He got tired of not being allowed to be serious when you got to be serious all the time, you replied. Damn it, do you really think that I am that shallow? That I only carry one emotion on my sleeve, at all times? That I don't have Desires, Hopes, Fears, and Sadness underneath the surface? Things are just as hard for me, you know.?

You paused and sat down at a random bench. And I sat down next to you. Our bags were strewn in every which direction. I looked at the busy people milling around, quickly trying to get to their gates, to their destinations. They didn't want to be here longer than they had to. We were in the middle of a Limbo Land. A place in between destinations. A place in between where the important moments in our life were supposed to take place.

We're not supposed to be discussing this here. We're supposed to be some place private and calm.

This is as calm as the world will ever be, you told me, as if I couldn't understand how frazzled the world already was, how we couldn't depend upon anything, not even a moment to ourselves to talk about being people any more. You got down on one knee in front of me. Listen to me. I love you. I want to be with you for the rest of my life. Will you please marry me?

But we still can't bring back the people that were killed by the Machine, I said sadly.

No. We can't, you told me. You got very red in the face and said under your breath John is never coming back. You paused for a moment. And got up. Embarrassed out of making a fool of yourself in front of all of these people walking from terminal to terminal. You thought that perhaps if I had said Yes, maybe the people would have clapped (maybe people would have seen you as a Hero in a Dreary World). Maybe. You wanted to reconcile what you had lost with me. You wanted to make up for my losses.

You said to me We can't bring back the dead, but we've created new life. We've made up for all the loss of life (without spending and losing more energy) threefold. We've tripled the world's population since the onset of loss of life due to the Machine. People will realize that there are other alternatives for energy. That Death isn't the answer.

...life into this world...

We should call our project the Life Machine, you said. We were lying on the sand, the March air clung to our bodies. It was cool, but not too cold. The sun warmed our faces. My head was on your chest and it bobbed up and down as you took in deep salty breaths. I rose with the waves. We lay on that same beach where all those people had died, staring out in our quest for Justice.

What? I didn't know what you were referring to at first.

Our Movement. We'll call it the Life Machine.

It rubbed me the wrong way, at first, like we were just supporting another Machine, another mechanical device, instead of merely endorsing Life Itself. But then I thought about Man and all his machines. How he needed them, now. Whether I liked it or not.

Fine then, I told you. Let's call it The Life Machine. I wasn't thinking about Names or Labels of what we were doing. I was thinking of the lives we had saved. I was thinking about the children who weren't dying of AIDS in Africa. I was not thinking about giving our work a name (something to call it in the History Books, something that would discredit the History Of Machinocide).

A shiver ran down the back of your spine, as if you suddenly let a million worries go, now that you had a name for what we had done, now that it all had some pretty bow to tie it up like a present. The Life Machine. The Life Machine. You seemed to repeat it in your mind constantly, until finally you just breathed one long sigh. It was done. It was done. We did well. I was so tired. I felt like I could sleep for days. Like I had missed a year of sleep or more. I just wanted to lay in bed and do nothing. Nothing. Not discuss the Accomplishments, the Greatest Achievements of our lives. I just wanted to lie down and relax.

Will you advertise the name for it? I asked you.

Maybe we should. It will be easier to get the word out. Enlighten our Cause. Cause some greater detriment to the Death Machine.

Alright, I said. I want it to have that.

I closed my eyes. Shielded myself from the cloudy sky. I wanted it to be spring again. I wanted it to be warm. You put a blanket around me and I just lay there, under the soft fabric. You placed your hands over my eyes and the sun had a blue glow.

You kissed my cheek and whispered in my ear ...marry me... marry me... you're the only one I could save the world with...

please... please... marry me.

I kissed you and I looked at you straight in the face. I want to have a life with you. I want to bring life into this world with you.

You have brought life into this world.

I want to bring our own life into this world.

I can't do that unless we're married, you said to me and looked away. No child wants a father that's not married to his mother. I want it to be Official. A *ketubah* and everything. You squeezed my right hip closer toward you. I want to be able to lie next to you in bed at night when we're old and be able to say This Is My Wife. I Love Her. We're Connected On Paper.

You rolled over toward me. I could see that you were tired. But that you weren't giving up on me.

Yes. I will marry you, I said to you finally. I want us, more than anything, to be connected on paper.

...autumn's carnage and winter's death...

I smelled flowers when we walked down the street in spring. Autumn's Carnage and Winter's Death passed. And even though the air was still chilly, it was a good chill. It opened our eyes and woke us up to the morning. I turned up my collar and shivered a little. I was glad the sun was coming out. You put your arm around my waist and told me our child would be born in early September. The flower blossoms on the trees fell from heaven like pink and orange confetti after a war. The colors filled every inch of the street, covering the black concrete. We were walking to the Supreme Court Building. Today was the day the Courts would announce that the *Machines were Unconstitutional Because They Killed, It Was Cruel And Unusual Punishment For Citizens, And Destroyed Our Liberties*. I remembered learning about the Bill Of Rights in High School. I remembered the black words on the white paper, and how it was hard sometimes for people to visualize how it influenced their lives. Now, it was directly impacting mine. Finally the government came through. Finally the people in power were starting to listen to the common people, clamoring for Freedom and Life.

The street was a little damp from the rain last night. The sun shone though the clouds and reflected onto the ground. It was as if we were stepping on heaven, blue sky below and above. As if we had somehow escaped from the hell we were once trapped in. The flower petals clung to the asphalt like Scratch And Sniff stickers. We were now in an Orchard Of Light And Nature, not the Artificial Bleak City. We were painting the world a new color. We redefined life. We were creating Postmodernism. We believed that it wasn't about Man. We had to let Morality, beyond human action, into our lives.

I didn't feel numb, anymore. I didn't feel empty.

How do you feel? I asked you, my arm holding tight to yours. I wondered if I could feel it from you, as if the emotion would seep out from your skin, as if I could smell it or taste it (as if it were somewhere oozing off of your aura). You just looked at me with crescent-eyed love, soaking in my smell, my touch, my gaze, as if memorizing all my past glances and summarizing them in this one spot, cementing them with this one breath of air that we took together.

You felt fulfilled. We felt it together. We felt the warmth consume us. This was fulfillment. Sufficiency. This was the best that life could offer us. It was as if something out of heaven came down and hugged us both. It's like when I was a child in my backyard, the sun beating down, warming me. A simple joy. Pleasures like lying in the grass, my hair tossing among the white daisies. Like I felt when I woke up next to you, your soft cheek near my chest. Like the smell of cinnamon. Like the softness of a rabbit's foot. I felt like I could run around for hours and not become tired. I felt like I just participated in a Protest, my lungs worn out from yelling. I felt like I just flew back in time to England and saw *Hamlet* being performed. Like the first time you kissed me. Like I'm keeping some secret about being Good from the rest of the world, but am too humble to state it outright. I just blushed and hummed sweet tunes to myself. I made up tunes that nobody has ever heard of, but that I love (that have been the soundtrack to my life). Music whispered in my ear. The Soundtrack To Life, playing over and over again. Reassuring me of the bliss of life. I felt. I felt! I was not some inanimate block of ice. You looked at me and placed your hand so gently behind mine (so tenderly, as if kissing it within your palm).

We walked to the same tune, you and I. It caught our breath and centered us. We were Together. We were One. Walking on the road. On this street. Did you feel it? Did you hear the music ringing? The rhythms made our eyes meet. The beat. Our heart drum synchronized. The melody pulsated throughout our bodies, from the top of our heads wet with dew to our frozen pale toes. I thought about what the Future had in store for us. Who knew? Maybe our children would have to fight the same madness we did. Maybe we would make sure that they never had to. I didn't know. I heard that summer here is beautiful, now that there will be people to live in it with us. People wouldn't kill each other, now. How could they? Their malicious taste buds would never be fed. They would never be stuffed, content with the sweet lingering flavor of Peace.

You told me you Don't miss the Old World. The New One is up to us to create and make better.

I wink at you and smile. Who said an Artist couldn't improve the world. Who said we couldn't save it? In the world of Sadism, we were Optimists. And we won. I love you. I love you. I love you.

Made in the USA